Brian Bouldrey

Love, the Magician

SR

CO~~MMENTA~~RIES,
EVA~~LUATIO~~NS . . .

D1637711

"B~~ouldrey's~~ *Love, the M*~~agician is~~ ~~o~~peratic in its pas-
sions, ~~expansive~~ in its themes of love,
mortal~~ity, and~~ the struggle to sus-
tain fai~~th, and~~ yet the author never
loses si~~ght of~~ his novel's human di-
mensions, ~~gi~~ving us fresh and memorable characters. This book is, to quote
the protagonist, Tristan Broder, `. . .
an awesomely dark story about a
prolonged mistake.' It is also a book
that sheds a bright, uncompromis-
ing light on one man's ~~encounter~~
with fate."

Bernard Cooper
Author of *Truth Serum*

~~Tristan~~ ~~Broder~~, the protagonist
~~1~~ and bereaved lover in Brian
Bouldrey's fine novel *Love, the Magician,* takes the reader on a curiously
unsettling pilgrimage into harsh terrain. Set in the Sonoran Desert during the Yacqui Deer Dance Easter
celebration, Tristan's journey to the
center of family, affection, grief, religion, and redemption reveals his
own prickly relationship toward being a survivor of `the Plague of the
Mon~~th~~.' This is a timely and
~~compelling story.~~"

~~___ ___son~~
~~Author of Nothi~~*ng to Tell*

More pre-publication
REVIEWS, COMMENTARIES, EVALUATIONS . . .

"Brian Bouldrey's writing is so smart, and so risky, and consistently carries that precarious, curious balance between humor and heartbreak. I'm never certain whether to bust out laughing or burst into tears. *Love, the Magician* is filled with examples of what its narrator calls `the little node of miracle that every human must have.' It's a really, really terrific novel."

Scott Heim
Author of *Mysterious Skin*
and *In Awe*

"Love, the Magician* is a modern-day pilgrimage to the intersection of love and death, faith and its loss, the rituals of worship and the rituals of pleasure. By turns comic and unsettling, lyrical and brutal, it is a tour de force of storytelling—a passionate voice in search of miracles."

Jean Thompson
Author of *Who Do You Love*

Southern Tier Editions
Harrington Park Press®
An Imprint of The Haworth Press, Inc.
New York • London • Oxford

Love, the Magician

HARRINGTON PARK PRESS
Southern Tier Editions
Gay Men's Fiction
Brian Bouldrey, Executive Editor

Love, the Magician by Brian Bouldrey

Distortion by Stephen Beachy

The City Kid by Paul Reidinger

Love, the Magician

Brian Bouldrey

Southern Tier Editions
Harrington Park Press®
An Imprint of The Haworth Press, Inc.
New York • London • Oxford

Published by

Southern Tier Editions, Harrington Park Press®, an imprint of The Haworth Press, Inc., 10 Alice Street, Binghamton, NY 13904-1580

PUBLISHER'S NOTE
This is a work of fiction. Names, characters, places, and incidents either are the products of the author's imagination or are used fictitiously, and any resemblance to actual persons, living or dead, business establishments, events, or locales is entirely coincidental.

Portions of this novel have appeared in *modern words* and *The James White Review.*

Cover design by Jennifer M. Gaska.

Cover photo © 1999 Bent Light.

Library of Congress Cataloging-in-Publication Data

Bouldrey, Brian.
    Love, the magician / Brian Bouldrey.
        p. cm.
    ISBN 1-56023-993-X (hc : alk. paper) — ISBN 1-56023-994-8 (pbk. : alk. paper)
    I. Title.

PS3552.O8314 L68 2000
813'.54—dc21

00-028183

For that other family I love—

Marta, Michael, and Rafaela:
No sorcerers, no magicians, no saints;
thank God.

Acknowledgments

Many people helped me write this book, in many ways. I would especially like to thank Paul Reidinger, Stephen Beachy, Gretchen Mazur, Michael Nava, Michael Lowenthal, and Miriam Wolf, and the entire staff of The Haworth Press, particularly Peg Marr, Bill Palmer, Bill Cohen, and Steve Zeeland.

Several books have also helped me discover the rich history of the Yaqui Nation, and all the native peoples of the Sonoran borderlands that give this tale its depth. In particular, I found the writing of William Griffith invaluable. His books *Beliefs and Holy Places* and *A Shared Space: Folklife in the Arizona-Sonora Borderlands* were extremely helpful. Griffith also plays a mean banjo. In addition, *A Yaqui Easter* by Muriel Thayer Panter, *Yaqui Myths and Legends* by Ruth Warner Giddings, and *Yaqui Deer Songs/ Maso Buikam: A Native American Poetry* by Larry Evers and Felipe S. Molina are excellent introductory books about the region. All of the above-mentioned books are not coincidentally published by the University of Arizona Press.

The Yaqui Nation, an extraordinary people and place straddling the United States and Mexican border in the lands called Sonora, are a source of great spiritual replenishment to me; they do not know me, but I've taken their example when I can in this life; I will always admire their dedication and resourcefulness, and strong sense of community. They are a great clan who have my highest respect.

You who do not have enchanted legs,
what are you looking for,
    what are you looking for?
You who do not have enchanted legs,
what are you looking for,
    what are you looking for?

You who do not have enchanted legs,
what are you looking for,
    what are you looking for?
You who do not have enchanted legs,
what are you looking for,
    what are you looking for?

You who do not have enchanted legs,
what are you looking for,
    what are you looking for?
You who do not have enchanted legs,
what are you looking for,
    what are you looking for?

Over there, in the middle
of the flower-covered wilderness,
        You who do not have enchanted legs,
what are you looking for,
    what are you looking for?
You who do not have enchanted legs,
what are you looking for,
    what are you looking for?

Yaqui Deer Song

El Amor Brujo (Love, the Magician) is the name of Manuel de Falla's ballet about Carmelo, a handsome man who has fallen in love with the gypsy beauty Candelas. Their romance is disturbed by the appearance of the spirit of Candelas's former lover, who died while they were betrothed.

De Falla composed his ballet in an atmosphere of ancient ceremony, evoking spirits that perform ritual fire dances and savage pagan rites. Candelas's phantom lover resorts to all kinds of spells in order to torment the living lovers. It is only when Lucía, another gypsy girl, manages to seduce the ghost that Carmelo and Candelas can end the sorcery and commit completely to their love.

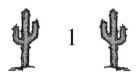

1

There is an unofficial saint in the Sonoran desert borderlands of Arizona and Mexico, named Jesús Malverde. He is the patron of the adolescents who live in the drainpipes of bordertown Nogales, the pushers and pimps and hustlers and addicts and other criminal elements. "Pray for us, Jesús Malverde." There are even prayer cards for him, the hanged man who intercedes on behalf of bad boys.

Tristan Broder, originally from Ontonagon, Michigan, where the view was blocked by lakes and forests, by the shores of Gitche Gumee, had come down into this alien landscape on Holy Thursday for a half-dozen reasons. To collect prayer cards of Malverde and other heretical figures was one of them.

Joe's sister, Maria, née, Jimenez, was an ex-Catholic Pentecostal convert and took a lot of pleasure helping in this and other searches. She'd practically planned this trip for Tristan. At the Phoenix airport, she stood next to him while the baggage carousel presented dozens of suitcases like possible game show prizes, and she chattered about what they needed to do in the next four days.

"It's perfect timing, you know, because the grass has grown completely over Joe's grave," she explained. "And you haven't seen the stone. The stone is real nice." Maria was never not upbeat. Upbeat people usually bothered Tristan, but Maria was a relief. When Joe and Tristan had been together, and Maria, in the ninth month of her pregnancy, left her first husband for another guy— for a truck driver, of all people—only Joe and Tristan would talk to her. For her second marriage to the truck driver, only Joe and Tristan sent a wedding gift, a big blue mixing bowl.

That was several years ago. The last time he'd seen her was at Joe's funeral, exactly four years past. Now it was late March but Arizona was hot. Some clown walked by Maria's pickup in the airport parking lot wearing a T-shirt showing a cactus and a skeleton simmering under the slogan, "Arizona: But It's A Dry Heat!"

Her truck was big and white. Pretty girls and pickup trucks, Tristan thought, they're so perfect together. But he realized that the truck was her husband's when he saw the two mirrored girls in silhouette, the half-reclined, buxom "player" emblem in duplicate, facing each other, one on each mudflap.

Maria explained, "It's Earl's. He said he'd watch the boys all weekend, so I could spend the whole time with you. What a guy." She watched Tristan study the silly silhouettes and pulled her own T-shirt tight to reveal her full, pretty, low-to-the-ground body. "Don't you think I look like the Mudflap Girl?"

She did! It almost redeemed Earl in Tristan's eyes, that he carried an image of his wife like his own religious icon wherever he went.

Once they got out on the open road, Tristan marveled at the desert. "God, what's that? A factory?" He pointed west of them, where at least seven brown plumes rose into the bleached-blue sky.

"Dust devils," she said. They looked diabolical, all right, like Japanese nuclear-waste-induced monsters burrowing into the earth to get at something or to escape. There were dozens of billboards along the way advertising developments of "adult communities." Tristan told Maria that in San Francisco, "adult" meant "Rated X." Here, it meant, "we prefer, in our golden years, not to be bothered by noisy children."

She laughed, but didn't pick up the thread. There should have been a ton to catch up on, yet they were both tired, and the heat that had leached the color from the sky also sapped their enthusiasm. The long Easter weekend ahead looked to Tristan like a huge over-catered banquet table spread, and he didn't know where to begin.

First, he had come to see where Joe had been buried. And then there was local color: he had come for those unofficial saints, to see their shrines. And perhaps the answer to the questions Why here?

and Why now? was the promise of the Yaqui Easter Ceremony, an epic Native American celebration of the Resurrection of Christ, complete with drums and dancing. And—oh yes—he wanted to see his in-laws. He'd always gotten along with them. And now they seemed all that was left of the physical existence of Joe. His mannerisms, his skin color, his very blood still embodied in their bodies—Maria's body, sitting right here next to him in the truck.

"Joe and I used to play a road game," he offered after a while. "I give you questions I just make up, and you just answer. It's easy."

"Like truth or dare?"

"No, easier. Like this: What's the best color for houses?"

"White."

He had a little notebook in his pocket. He decided to write down all her answers, like he was taking a survey. "Halloween, Thanksgiving, or Christmas?"

"Christmas!"

"Childhood nickname?"

"La Chupapinga."

"That's so funny—that was mine, too. Favorite food smell?"

"Baking bread."

"Death or taxes?"

"Taxes."

"Devil or the Deep Blue Sea?"

"Deep Blue Sea."

"Scalloped, mashed, or baked?"

"French fries."

"First name of the person you hate most in the world."

"Debbie."

"Name you would have if you were a boy."

"Joe."

He looked over at her. The truck window was open and her chestnut hair was flying all over the place.

"Are we going straight to the graveyard?" Tristan wanted to know when they saw the Tucson City Limit signs.

She shook her head, concentrating on her exit. "I hope that's okay. Dinner with Mom. But even before that, I told Mik we'd meet him at El Tiradito."

"El Tiradito?"

"The wishing shrine. Since you're on a quest for folklore saints, he's the best place to start." She told him about the bandit who'd been shot for true love a hundred years ago, and the shrine of candles that had persisted at the location ever since. If you lit a candle at the bandit's shrine and it burned all night, you got your wish.

While she navigated the freeway, he stole little peeks at her, trying, as usual, to see if she looked like her dead brother. Of course she did. The obviousness was kind of disappointing. What he thrilled to was when she said something the way Joe had said it, held out the word "wissshhhing," enjoying the "sh" blend. Or when her voice squeaked with enthusiasm.

Sometimes he did the mental equivalent of squinting his eyes, to pretend he didn't know her. *La Chupapinga?* Who would ever guess that the Mudflap Girl behind the wheel of this truck was a fervent Pentecostal, with a brother dead to the Plague of the Morally Lazy in the late twentieth century?

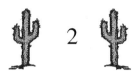 2

Mik was waiting by the shrine when they pulled in. He had been Joe's best friend when he lived here near his family. Mik was a short, slightly tubby Punjabi guy whose only departure from humility was his mane of silky black hair. For years, Tristan had assumed that Joe and Mik had been lovers early on, one of those stalled-out things that rolled over into friendship. Tristan never brought it up with Joe, out of some respect for the past. But somewhere along the way—yes, on a road trip to the border on one of those early visits—Tristan discovered that Mik wasn't even gay. All the idiosyncrasies of retaining his own culture: buttoned-down shirts, bowing toward Mecca, fasting during Ramadan, an avoidance of sexual direction—Tristan had mistaken Mik's bentness for his own sort.

And with the strict Muslim observance of temperance and sexual abstinence and also a might-as-well-be vegetarianism, Mik's lifestyle jibed oddly well with Maria's clean Pentecostal living. They'd become very close.

Mik was standing next to a brick-and-adobe wall that might have been mistaken for the remains of a house that had burned to the ground, the side with the chimney remaining standing. The wall was scalloped up into a curl like the shape of saloon doors in the Wild West. Flickering candles twittered around him, but he was alone at the open-air shrine. He waved to their car.

"It's something, isn't it?" Mik said when Tristan got out.

Tristan hugged him. "How are you?"

"My parents have moved back to India," he said. "One by one, everybody's going away."

Maria said, "Hey, what am I, chopped liver?"

"Wow, moved back, just like that," said Tristan. He knew of the illiterate laborers Mik had come from, who'd emigrated bizarrely to Arizona, worked as sharecroppers (mistaken for Mexicans) and amassed money to send Mik to college; Mik was in historic preservation now, and though he didn't make a bundle, even his parents understood it to be solid, respectable work. In the ride from the airport, Maria told Tristan how Mik's office had helped save El Tiradito from a freeway expansion plan.

Tristan could tell that Maria was better at telling Mik's parents' story than Mik himself, and knew the ontological doodads necessary to make it a story: "They're considered wealthy, now," she explained, and Mik let her. "Aristocracy. And to have had such an adventure in American cowboy country, bang bang! You can imagine how popular. And a son with an education, smart and handsome—"

"—and unmarried," added Mik.

"Think of the possibility," Maria mended the lament. "The handsome Raj looking for his perfect princess." She turned to Tristan again. "And—" she grabbed his arm, the this-is-the-best-part gesture, "—and—they have a pet monkey."

Tristan loved that. "A monkey! What's its name?"

Mik shrugged. Tristan could see that the best part of the story for the Americanos was the dullest for the Punjabi: "I don't know. When they want it, they just yell, 'Hey, Monkey!' "

Maria and Tristan thought this was hysterical.

"Mik's parents loved Joe," Maria said.

Mik picked up a sack that he'd nestled between his two shoes. He pulled out candles, big ones poured into long jars, decorated with Hispanic pictures of saints.

"Joe was one of the few people who'd hang around with me," Mik said.

Tristan wouldn't say it out loud, but looking now at Maria and Mik, he saw that they could have been twins, dark-skinned, dark-haired. It wouldn't be right to say so. Why was it that you could compliment a cultural group—the English are so resourceful, the French make great cheese, gays have nice sweaters—but that's as far as it went. Oh yes!—they could all laugh at the ridiculousness of white guys like Tristan who wanted to give a wild monkey a name—for that's how whitey conquered the world: with names. With Maria and Mik (and if Joe were around, him too), Tristan was the outsider, the nonmember.

Mik handed Maria a candle, and she rolled her eyes. "Maria thinks it's all voodoo," Mik said to Tristan.

"But I'll do it anyway—it can't hurt, can it?" She pulled out a cigarette lighter and handed it to Mik first. "What you do is make a wish. If it burns all night, it will come true."

"I'll wish for something small, like—"

"You can't tell! It's like a birthday wish. It won't come true if you tell."

Tristan watched her scrunch up her eyes like a child over a cake. Whatever she wished, she wanted it badly, ferociously. Tristan hoped it wasn't one of those horrid monkey's paw kinds of wishes—wishing the dead back to life and hearing a subsequent horrible knock on the door on a stormy night. He was at a loss what to wish for. The wish he'd wanted most had been recently granted, and now he didn't know what to do with the grant. Nevertheless, he scrunched his eyes, too, and lit. All three of them placed their candles against a wall blackened by waxy smoke, where the wind was least likely to blow them out.

"It's not so much that I believe it'll come true," Maria said. "I'd just hate to come back here and find out my candle had blown out and I'd been selected as a person denied my wish. That would seem bad to me."

Just then, a sedan full of old Hispanic ladies pulled into the lot next to them. There were four, no, five, and they were playing wobbly polka-sounding Mexican oompah music very loud. They swarmed out like clowns from a circus car and commandeered the wishing shrine. They gathered up burned out candles and swept away ash.

They rearranged two wrought iron stands that held the long jars and tidied some plastic flowers, long-faded by the Arizona sun. One arranged stones in a circle. Then, another took a tall glass that was virtually all molten wax, and spilled it on the sand around a group of seven candles, creating a magic circle. The chief madre of the group made the paraffin burn in the sand, like Loki's magic

fire around Brünnhilde. The gesture had the flair of the mythological. When Tristan came up close, he saw it wasn't a circle but a
valentine heart, and the flames in the sand licking at the candle jars
caused them to melt and the glass began cracking. One of the candles drowned itself out in the molten wax.

That's when Maria surprised Tristan by springing up to the
ladies. *"Oigan, señoras!"* she charged. *"¿Cuál es el problema?"*
Tristan knew enough Spanish to understand, but not enough to
intervene. Foreign languages held a spell over him, rendered him a
zombie.

The madre of madres argued with Maria. "We are uniting our
wishes to make them more powerful. We are hoping that my
daughter and her son will fall in love. It's very important."

"But don't you see what you're doing? These candles are going
out in the heat of your fire. Now, all the people who lit them won't
get their wish." As if to punctuate her protest, one of the candles in
the contained inferno cracked. Glass blackened among the flames.

"Mind your own business," *la madrina* shrieked back. "We
have suffered long enough, *mi vida*."

Maria scooped up sand in her hands and doused a portion of the
magic flaming heart. It was like putting a stick into a nest of
hornets. The señoras screeched and nattered and one grabbed
Maria's arm.

That's when Mik stepped up and said, "That's enough." He
shuffled both Maria and Tristan over to his car. The women shook
their fists behind them like villagers out to pitchfork Frankenstein.

"Jesus loves you!" Maria called out the window as they drove
away. Tristan looked at her: is that how Pentecostals behaved? But
the urge to laugh won out. And they all did.

Maybe Maria was acting in an un-Christian manner for Tristan's
benefit. After all, Joe had announced his own atheism to his sister
and mother in the presence of Tristan. He'd walked into his
mother's house and pointed at the severe crucifix over the couch
and shrieked, "Mom! Who's that dead man hanging in the living
room?" Maria probably thought Joe's atheism was Tristan's fault.

Soon they were out of sight. "Superstitious old bags," she
seethed. It took them a long car ride around town before she could

talk about anything else. "I'm sorry, Tristan," she kept saying. "I'm giving you a bad impression on your first night, but they made me so mad."

"I know, I know," Tristan said. And he did.

Mik said, "We'll come back for your truck later. Mrs. Jimenez is waiting on us for dinner." Mik always addressed Joe's and Maria's mother in this way, cordially, never on a first-name basis. To Tristan, it didn't sound polite so much as standoffish.

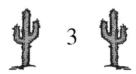

3

Mrs. Jimenez owned a row of attached adobes in the *barrio histórico,* lived in the first one and rented the other three as bed-and-breakfast rooms. She kept a locally famous garden and her cheerfulness—inherited by her daughter and son, too—suited her role as innkeeper.

It was after dark, and the three floodlights that illuminated the adobe outside gave the place a warm yet lonely feeling. There was a placard in the window of the door, showing the Virgin of Guadalupe and the words, in Spanish: "This house is Catholic. We don't accept the propaganda of other religions."

Maria did the eye roll, but smiled at the same time. "She put that up for my benefit."

Before anybody could knock, Mrs. Jimenez was at the portal. "Tristan!" she said, and hugged him close. She'd been gardening, and smelled of dust when it's been watered with a hose. "It's been so long. You look so good; I'm so happy. Well fed, good."

"You look good too, Mrs. Jimenez," Tristan said, but he decided she had the face of an aging opera diva, full of big mugging versions of feelings. Also, her hair had withstood a lifetime of getting "done," and now seemed matted, almost like a wig. The skin around her eyes and lips was red and swollen from applying and scrubbing off makeup. She *was* a diva, too old for the romantic roles, a Fricka, maybe, though not even a Marschallin in *Rosenkavalier* anymore.

How strange, Tristan thought, that he'd begun to be interested in opera again, after several years of avoiding it. He was lately able to bear those broad swathes of emotion, oddly understandable despite their foreign tongues.

Mrs. Jimenez ushered the three of them in. Dinner was on the table. "What time did you get in?" she asked, which meant, somehow, "This table has been ready for half an hour; what has kept it waiting?" Which meant, "What kept *me* waiting?"

Maria said, "We took him over by El Tiradito first, to light a candle."

Mrs. Jimenez was thrilled. All was forgiven. "A lovely idea. Was it yours, Maria?" she asked her Pentecostal daughter hopefully.

"No, Mik wanted to see the placard again, since he helped save it, you know."

Tristan volunteered, "And Maria saved our wishes from being ruined by witchy old ladies." Maria shot him a look that let him know, *no más,* he'd made a mistake.

"Oh?" said Mrs. Jimenez. She was serving up what were obvious leftovers from her bed-and-breakfast meals: four quiches, a basket of poppyseed muffins, sausages, salsa. Tristan liked this. "Pass me your plate, Mik. There's juice and coffee on the counter, help yourself," she said. Then, "What happened?"

Since the cat was out of the bag, Tristan told her everything that occurred at the wishing shrine and then, to defuse the inevitable argument between mother and daughter, posed the situation as a moral puzzle: "What's the right thing to do, if we have to choose between respecting our elders and stopping wrongdoing?"

Such a good peacekeeper. But Tristan had nothing to worry about, for he was in a room full of peacekeepers: the Catholic innkeeper, the Pentecostal, the gentle Punjabi cipher, and he himself who always searched into the character of even the crappiest people for the little node of miracle that every human must have.

No, no argument would occur here; Mrs. Jimenez's first input was all reconciliation. "As an elder expecting respect, I don't think I deserve it unless I show respect myself. If these ladies couldn't respect others' wishes, then they got what they deserved." She turned to Maria. "I'm just so afraid you're going to go after the wrong person one of these days, and some *chola* will stick you with a stiletto."

Mrs. Jimenez kept her bed-and-breakfast at the edge of an iffy neighborhood. There were bars on the windows facing the street, and next door was a grocery store that would sell you a single cigarette and was popular among truckers because it had a parking lot big enough to turn rigs around.

Maria got up and kissed her mother.

"Have you been to Joe's grave yet?" Mrs. Jimenez asked. "There's been a lot of work done since you last saw it."

All the work, in fact. The last time he saw it, the box of Joe's ashes was being placed in a hole by two bewildered altar boys beside the long, tall, scared priest, Father Dolan. It was Joe's last magic trick, to disappear into thin air. His audience stood gaping at the grave. It took years for magic like that to dissipate. Mrs. Jimenez had, well, completely fallen apart. She'd gone to her knees and reached into the hole and had to be pulled back by Maria and Mik and Tristan.

"What have you done out there?" Tristan asked politely.

Mother and daughter glanced at each other.

"Well, Tristan," Mrs. Jimenez said. "Now don't be upset. But every year you were sending me those checks on Valentine's Day and asking me to put down roses for him. It was a lovely gesture, honey, but those roses didn't last more than three days before they dried up and looked like hell. So two years ago, I started a garden. I put in some local plants, a brittle bush, rose mallow, like that. Every year I plant something new." She showed her teeth to Tristan, clenching them, bracing them for impact and Tristan's disappointment.

Tristan said, "That's a brilliant idea! I wish I'd thought of it myself but I figured a project like that would be a lot of work."

"I don't mind it," said Mrs. Jimenez. "Gives me work to do when I'm out there."

During some past phone call, Maria had told Tristan her mother was out there all the time. Her husband's grave looked neglected next to Joe's pampered stone.

"Good quiche, Mrs. Jimenez," said Mik.

"It's vegetarian," she reassured him.

There was a clicking and scratching on the back screen door. It was Murphy, the moppy little mutt Mrs. Jimenez had found in the desert six years ago, and adopted. Maria yelled, "Hey, Monkey!" and was delighted when Murphy trundled directly to her. Around his neck was a burden of tags that reminded Tristan of a janitor's key ring: his vaccination records, a license, a cabochon with an "M," a tag with the B and B's number and address, and a medallion of San Martin des Porres, patron saint of hobos and lost souls. *"RUEGA POR NOSOTROS."*

"I've poured so much money into Murphy," Mrs. Jimenez said, after a sigh. "He's my million-dollar dog." "Murphy" was short for Murphy's Law. "It's the money I should have been spending on Joe, but he was up there with you in San Francisco and you had it all under control. I didn't know what to do with myself. A mother has those instincts, you know. Murphy'd be dead by now if I didn't have anything to do with those instincts."

The path to Joe's death had not, in fact, been smooth, but muddled in the way of all chronic sickness. On four occasions, Tristan had called Mrs. Jimenez secretly on the cordless phone at its fuzzy extreme out in the yard where he mumbled, "Can you hear me? Better come, I think this is it," only to watch Joe rally yet again, the mission scuttled.

There wasn't a strain between mother and son, but Joe was so terribly embarrassed by his physical decrepitude, he didn't want her to see what remained of him. That's why he demanded cremation; that's why, Tristan was convinced, Joe must've overheard one of the secret garden phone calls because he died, suddenly, two days before Mrs. Jimenez was scheduled to arrive by plane.

She never did see her son in those last stages, the dwindling, drawn, ashen version of her son. For so long, Tristan was pleased at this—let her remain with the illusion of a whole man who had walked into a box and vanished, rather than the diminished master. Lately, though, Tristan had been changing his mind.

"What are you thinking about?" asked Mrs. Jimenez softly. Apparently, there had been a long silence over the table. Maria fed Murphy a sausage bit. Murphy was known to eat anything that hit the floor.

"That Joe was a magician. Or a saint. A wizard. Something like that."

Mik said, "I remember the first time I met him, he was working on the Congress Hotel. I walked by and he was on his lunch hour, but instead of whistling at girls with the other guys, he was messing around with some wire and a screwdriver. I said, 'What are you doing?' and he said, 'I'm making a lamp.' Making a lamp? What does that mean? Nobody makes a lamp."

They all giggled. It was true. Joe was an electrician, and he could work wonders with wires. He was Reddy Kilowatt, that zippy trademark guy made of lightning bolts with a light bulb for a head and sockets for ears: "I work for pennies a day!" He was Thor with a mighty hammer, ushering the gods into Valhalla. Hei-da, hei-da, hei-do!

Tristan had fallen in love with that power, all the magic of harnessed science: passion *was* reason. Give Joe a fulcrum and lever and a place to stand, and he could have moved the world.

"He was so generous," Tristan said. "He'd find broken clocks or toasters and fix them and then just give them away."

"The miracles of the saints," Maria said. They'd been through this hagiography business before. She didn't believe that saints had any special divine powers, and felt no sense of sacrilegiosity by merrily listing her own brother's miracles that would elect him into the holy elite: "the miracle of the making of the lamp, a new miracle."

Tristan noticed that Mrs. Jimenez was going to fall apart again, the way she had at the cemetery years ago. She got up to bring dishes to the sink. "Maria, why don't you show Tristan his room," she said. And then to Tristan: "I've put you in the end unit, if that's okay, for privacy. I've only got one guest coming this week—I decided to take it easy this weekend and told all callers I was completely booked."

Without a word or waiting for Maria to catch up, he stood and slipped out the back door and into the garden, which was mostly invisible in the dark. Yet he could smell the moistness and see that he was surrounded by agapanthus, the same plants that his own mother mollycoddled, busing them in and out of her house so they wouldn't freeze in Michigan winters. But here in the West, they thrived like weeds in the little corners of gas stations and along roads.

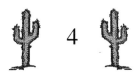

4

Tristan's rooms were exactly like Mrs. Jimenez's, a full kitchen and dining nook, bedroom, and living room all shotgun style, adobe. The thick walls were covered with Native American rugs and old photos. There was a mint on the pillow and melon-colored glycerin soaps in the bathroom, a coffee pot of his own with crummy grounds in silver jet packs, and stacks of tourist brochures.

Maria showed him everything and how it worked, even though he already knew—he'd been here half a dozen times with Joe. She went back to eat and console her mother. He was let alone for a few minutes to unpack, but Murphy stayed with him, which was pretty nice of the mutt, since Tristan didn't have any food to be begged for. He pulled out the big white plastic bottle of all the pills, mixed together: he chose three blue ones, one brick-red capsule, one little white diamond that looked like the French Bar-Tabac signs he'd seen when roving alone, a widower, through that country. They went down the hatch twice daily and that was that. According to his doctor's blood workups, the medicine worked. But it was all numbers for Tristan, theoretical health like a cellophane keeping fresh the real goods of real health. He let himself wonder now and then whether this weren't a big medical establishment joke, a study of positive thinking.

Here they were: the future, a long-lengthened road of tablets and capsules, more magic for Tristan to deal with. Why did he feel so ungrateful? He was going to live, at least a lot longer than he'd anticipated. After a year he was just beginning to let it sink in. He'd have to plan for the future.

He'd been living by the seat of his pants, always no savings, no retirement fund, no skin care, for God's sake, none of it seeming necessary. He'd been living this way for years now, first when he'd been swept into the Liebestod of his love for Joe, the "I can't live without you" of it, and then the veiled careless plunge of bereavement, where he cared even less for a Joeless future.

The pills were a nuisance to remember to take with food, and there were dangers almost fabulous attached to them, admonitions out of a fairy tale. "But if you dare once to take them without food, then the absorption will not take effect." Or, "And if you are ever to stop taking them for but a day, the virus, which, like evil, can be held at bay yet is never vanquished, will learn how to overcome the magical elixir, and the potion will be rendered useless." Or more simply: "Beware cross-resistance!"

Still, if Joe were here now, Tristan thought, the thing that would piss him off the most would be finding out how little trouble these pills gave Tristan. Tristan remembered Joe's endless trips to the doctor for any number of prophylactics, inhaling Bactrim to avoid pneumocystis, the experimental stuff, the rotgut AZT, the experiment with photography chemicals, the wild goose chase looking for a blood change, chemotherapy, respirators, antifungals, procedures of all sorts, all of these as poisonous as the AIDS that eventually ate Joe alive. The headaches, the stomachaches, the diarrhea, the mood shifts, the drowsiness.

And this, this handful of nuisance, did its work on Tristan invisibly. This new protocol was clean as a whistle. Not even diarrhea for Tristan. Just as long as he took the pills with food and faced the inconvenience of remembering them twice a day. In fact, he swore they energized him a little each time he took them.

He drew a glass of water. One of the pills, because he was always sort of a klutz, dropped onto the adobe floor. Murphy scuttled up to it, sniffed it, and left it alone.

"That's right," said Tristan. "It's miracle medicine. It isn't natural. They don't occur in our environment, and even little dogs know that." He swallowed the pills, chugged the water. "But I've heard about you, Murphster; they say you'd eat rancid lard if it dropped on the floor."

Murphy realized there was to be no food from this quarter, and trotted back out into the garden and perhaps to do a little triage work with those who were eating real food and might share it.

"I'll only let you down, Mr. Murph," Tristan called after him.

On the nightstand was yet another photo of Joe and Tristan together, part of the turn-down service, it seemed, along with the soaps and mints. Tristan picked it up. "Look how much hair I've lost," he wondered. "Look how much weight I've put on." He felt momentarily guilty looking at himself in the picture and not at Joe, but how could he not be distracted by this—this *phenomenon:* four years and Joe was still the same, and always would be, perpetually thirty years old while Tristan grew older and older. One of Tristan's self-indulgences was fantasizing about Joe simply returning one day out of the blue from some cryogenic sleep, and their resuming the relationship. How long before their growing age difference would render any thought of resuming the relationship unseemly? No doubt Joe would look at Tristan's paunch and turn up his nose. "But my eyes are still blue, the way you liked them," Tristan said to the photo. "My brow still furrows that way, I still make that involuntary rabbit sniff with my nose, I'm still the lipless wonder, hair still grows out of my ears and needs trimming, and nobody, nobody is here to do it."

In the photo, they were both in tuxedos. Joe had sent it to his mother when the two had been domestically partnered, mostly to torment her. Joe reported that his mother thought they were "making a mockery of the sacrament." She didn't understand that ironically, Joe, who'd decided the Church was a vicious anachronism, took the ceremony with dead seriousness.

If anybody had mocked the ceremony, it had been Tristan. At the time, he could tell that Joe was slowing down, his T-cell count on its way toward zero and his persistent cough a cliché of ominousness. Joe had been hinting at the partnership. When Tristan suggested they go to city hall, Joe cried.

They took a handful of friends downtown and drank champagne on the steps. A friend made it into a home movie. Tristan's fondest memory was the moment on the videotape when, in close-up, Joe loosened the wire fastening on a new bottle of bubbly and the cork sailed out. Joe watched the trajectory of the thing as it took a per-fect shot at a gawking tourist; nothing could have been better planned—the pantomime, the eyes bugging out in horror, and then the earnest face as a policeman approached and spoke, off-screen, telling them all to move along now.

And then, afterward, after the documents were signed and the flowers were lavished and the Rice-A-Roni thrown at the depart-ing lovers, there was the party. Everybody, it seemed to Tristan, took the thing seriously except him. When he jokingly told friends that their pattern was "Blue Willow," they received more than a full set of the stuff, as well as other beautiful things, earnest gifts—even toasters. Remembering this, Tristan wondered whether this embarrassment of riches came before or after the shipment of the blue bowl to Maria and Earl.

And after Joe died, so many of these things sat in boxes unused. Three toasters. Tristan never threw them away. They sat in the basement with the cuckoo clock, the work clothes, the electri-cian's manuals, the tools.

And then one day, after a long trip to Europe, Tristan had come home and realized how well he'd lived with just a suitcase full of things, and how many times he thought of Joe without the help of the mementos, and said out loud, in the basement, "A toaster is not Joe; a toaster is a toaster," and ruthlessly packed all of it up and sent it to Community Thrift.

What little remained was in this bag he'd brought with him, gifts for the family: some of Joe's personal things, not toasters. But lately—and this was the problem—all of it had suddenly lost that magical power. Tristan remembered a poem about how Rob-inson Crusoe had prayed every day for his knife not to break, but after he was rescued, it became a useless museum piece.

Well, not all of it was useless. He clung very closely to the cane Joe had made for himself out of a piece of copper pipe and fit-tings—perhaps because Tristan might one day use it, too. Or the rosewood cabinet full of mah-jongg tablets in ivory, three pieces missing and therefore unusable, or the wooden statue of a deer, with one antler broken. These he wouldn't give away. Couldn't.

Something had snapped since the new drug protocol kicked in. Tristan was afraid it was mere savage glee. But this knife, this jacket, these handmade sconces he pulled out of his bag and put into a paper sack, they'd grown cold, inert, when only a year ago they had been things to grasp at and beg to.

5

When he returned to the Jimenez unit, they were all shaking their heads. "Science, technology, progress," Mik lamented. Tristan might have worried that somebody had eavesdropped on his pill-taking, but he knew in a moment that they were talking about the mass suicide that had occurred the day before.

"How could anyone just blindly follow a joker like that?" Maria said, holding up a picture of the pop-eyed cult leader on the front page of a newspaper.

"Maybe he didn't always bug his eyes out," Tristan said. "Maybe that's what fooled them." Everybody turned around at his reentry into the room and the conversation, but they were on to something, and no wisecrack could stop the momentum of this dinnertime inquiry.

Mrs. Jimenez said, "I heard some of their friends and family interviewed on CNN. They didn't even seem to care. It's no wonder."

"What if it's true, though?" said Tristan. "What if they really did get in the spaceship behind the comet? There have been so many portents in the sky lately."

Dust devils—and just three days ago, he'd watched a lunar eclipse. The strength of it had surprised him, the quality of the velvety inked-out moon's remaining light was concentrated metallic, the kind of light that glinted off a table knife, or spoon, during a candlelight dinner.

Mik said, "People feel so lost these days."

"Yes," said Tristan. "Nobody knows what's going to happen. My students only want to read novels about the turn of the nine-

teenth century, or science fiction." Tristan taught English literature at City College.

For dessert there was fresh fruit, big bowls of chopped-up
grapefruit sprinkled with powdered sugar. "From my garden!"
said Mrs. Jimenez. "So juicy I've had to eat them over the sink."

"What have you got there in the bag?" Maria asked Tristan.

"Gifts," said Tristan. He pulled things out. For Mik, he had the
Swiss Army knife, one of the ridiculous ones with scissors and
toothpicks and awls. He handed the jacket to Maria, embroidered
with little studs and glitter. For Mrs. Jimenez, he pulled out the
two wall sconces for candles. "Joe made these. They all belonged
to Joe. I've been hoarding his stuff for so long I couldn't let any of
it go. And I didn't know what you would want of his, what would
be most useful to you."

"Yes," Mik said, "gifts can be inefficient." Tristan scrutinized
Mik scrutinizing the knife. Did he think it was silly? Was it worse
than inefficient—inappropriate? He'd heard how some cultures
considered it bad luck to give knives as gifts.

He looked over at Maria. Maybe they were all still trying to
avoid the emotional moment that had been welling up just before
he'd gone to his rooms. Was Maria upset that Tristan might bring
her mother close to that moment again, after it seemed to have
blown over?

But Mrs. Jimenez didn't cry; she was studying her gift. "If it
belonged to Joe, then that's good enough," she said.

It didn't look as if Maria liked her jacket, either, because she put
it into her lap after thanking Tristan, a quick assessment. There
was a round of thanks and Tristan said, "It's another step." Then
they were quiet for a while, cleaning up.

Tristan was relieved of dishwashing duty because he stacked
plates and glasses precariously on the drying rack. After one near
disaster, Mik took the towel out of Tristan's hand. Tristan bided
his time drinking wine and asking Tucson questions.

"Are we finished here?" asked Maria. "Because I want to go
pick up my truck at the wishing shrine and I want Tristan to see
some of the Easter Ceremony tonight."

The Yaqui ceremony—which had begun days ago and was going on even as they sat here in the peaceful Tucson evening, was known to Tristan only from what Joe had lackadaisically described of it. Hundreds of years before, missionaries came to this part of Sonora to convert the natives to Catholicism. The Yaqui had invited the Jesuits into their land after they defeated the Spanish. They consented to conversion, but since the Yaqui were such a remote people, it was difficult to establish the strict catechism of worship, although all the Yaqui towns were mission towns. The Yaqui took what they liked or remembered of the Catholic liturgy but also retained several of their own traditional beliefs, cooking up a mythological mish-mash sure to make the Pope's head spin. But who could dare squelch the rich and monumental pageant of the Yaqui Easter? Every member of the reservation would play a part in the story of Christ's death and Resurrection, which never ended, round the clock.

Why was Tristan fascinated by these proceedings? Was it simply because he felt there was no role, post-Joe, post-AIDS, for himself? The Yaqui were poor, lived cooped up on dusty reservations. Tristan lived in San Francisco, in a boom economy. The Yaqui shared and overlapped. People like Tristan could afford to be alone.

Mrs. Jimenez sighed. "Oh, that endless thing? I don't know how much you care, Tristan, but from one Catholic to another, there's a lot of rules being broken up there at Old Pascua Village."

The turning point in Tristan's relationship with Mrs. Jimenez, after she first found out that he was bedding down with her son and "making a mockery" of the sacrament of marriage, was when she called up San Francisco one Sunday to argue. "Where's Tristan?" she had asked Joe when their fight had reached a dead end. "I want to talk to him."

"You can't," Joe had said.

"Why not? Is he afraid of me? You know I'm polite with strangers. I just want to talk to him."

"He's not here. He's . . . . " When Joe reported this conversation, he said that he'd slurred the last part in embarrassment, so she had to ask again.

"He's where?"

"He's at church."

After that, she always hoped Tristan would be a good influence on her wayward son.

Tristan never attempted to explain his lingering irrational attraction to Catholicism. But when he met Joe and found out he was HIV positive, Tristan would go into a church and beg like a teenager in his prayers, striking one-sided deals with the Lord: give me five good years with him and I'll be celibate for the rest of my life. Give me ten years and I'll become a priest afterward.

Had he waffled? No, the Lord had done the waffling. Tristan had gotten four years with Joe, and two of those were one infection after another.

And during the sickness, Tristan's prayers were surprisingly not of the deal-making variety, but of the wish for peace. An endless round of Franciscan Prayers and Canticles to the Sun and All Will Be Wells.

And after all the dealmaking, the dying, then what kept Tristan Catholic? Sociological curiosity. Maybe he was trying to feel superior, regain some dignity by observing the unofficial santos of Sonora, watching all the wishes and petitions, watching himself in a previous life, since his should have ended back there.

Or maybe he was just jealous—could people still believe anything? Did the Yaqui?

Another unofficial saint, besides Jesús Malverde and El Tiradito, was Juan Soldado. There were many versions of Soldado's legend, but the theme was always the same. He was a young army private whose commanding officer raped and murdered a little girl when she came to the garrison with laundry. The *capitan* then accused Juan Soldado of the horrible crime, and the recruit was executed without trial. He began appearing as a spirit, first to his mother keeping vigil, then to other women at the site of his death, and later to others.

There would have been a church at Soldado's grave, but the priests would not allow it to be built. Instead, there is a chapel made of tattered scraps of lumber, covered with testimonials, thanking him for getting a man out of prison, ridding a child of mental illness.

Tristan could easily imagine Mrs. Jimenez affixing a folded paper note to the makeshift shrine with a thumbtack.

"The Yaqui break rules, but so do we," said Tristan to Mrs. Jimenez, and then he corrected himself to soften the observation: "So do I. Has El Tiradito received a blessing from the Church?"

Mrs. Jimenez scooped up Murphy, and let him lick her cheek. "The Church has not recognized the wishing shrine, because the wishing shrine does not grant wishes."

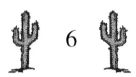

6

They never made it to Old Pascua Village for the ceremonies that night. What happened was that Mik suggested they go up Tumamoc Hill to see the comet. In San Francisco, the city lights had been so bright nothing celestial could really be seen.

Tristan didn't expect much. He'd grown up with the overzealous promise of Kahoutek. He'd watched Halley's fizzle. This Hale-Bopp was an afterthought, casually mentioned on public radio's *Star Date* and considered a minor phenomenon. That thirty-nine lost souls had ended their lives over the comet added a certain dimension of the grand and pathetic.

So when Mik let the car joggle up the side of the hill (obviously a primo make-out zone and, judging from the inscrutable graffiti, the site of gang warfare) and casually pointed up through the windshield, Tristan squealed, "My God, stop the car."

For Tristan, it was immense. Brighter than any star or planet in this spangled desert sky. Behind its pulsing head was the tail, the sparkly milky smear of detritus that, unless his eyes were deceiving him, flared up and burned back now and then. It blazed above him like something out of a glitter-adorned kitsch Christmas card. "It's a miracle," he gasped again.

Mik wasn't as impressed. "It's just a star with a smudge behind it."

"If I were a Wise Man, I would have followed it," Tristan contended.

The car was parked behind a low rider full of *cholo* boys. Mik and Maria wanted to move farther up. Tristan was too taken with the comet to worry. "Can we go somewhere where we can just sit and watch it?"

Maria suggested the cemetery.

"I had something to put on the grave," Tristan said, thinking of an item he had, sitting in his pack at the adobe. "But I guess I can come back again later."

Mik drove them to the edge of town. It turned out to be a good place to see the comet; they could turn their backs on Tucson's lights and there it was, persisting. That's the word, Tristan thought, it persists.

The neighborhood near the cemetery was very nice. Maria giggled. "When we were teenagers, we'd sneak out to go to the clubs. We'd put on our nicest clothes and shiny shoes and I'd put on lots of makeup. We had fake IDs, but we didn't have any money for the cover charge. So Joe used to take me around here in his Chevette and walk up to total strangers and say, 'Hello, my friend,'—he'd say it that way, like he ran a 7-Eleven or something. They'd say hello and he'd say, 'We've got a little project. You see, this girl has just been crowned princess of the town, and now she needs to purchase all the things suitable for a princess—you know, dress, shoes, crown. And so we need your cooperation.' "

Tristan laughed. Joe had never told him that story before. "Did it work?"

"Only with the Latinos," she said. "Joe knew Spanish as a second language. He told me he didn't feel like he was lying so much when he was speaking Spanish because it all felt artificial. And they were so proud that the princess of the town was a Latina." Maria made a motion with the flat of her hand under the tips of her hair as if she were fluffing a complex hairdo—even though her hair was silky-straight.

Tristan rewarded her with a gift easy to give: "He would've done anything for you."

As they drove on into the night, he tried to memorize the path Mik made to the cemetery plot: two lefts, one right, another left—but there was a wide arcing bend that really wasn't a turn, so he suddenly stopped paying attention. It was too much fun watching the comet above, its flagrant end-of-the-world absurdity.

Mik parked the car and they got out and Mik said, "Graveyards are spooky when you don't know anybody dead. Then they're just sad." He was prepared. He had a flashlight.

Maria agreed, earnestly. "Yeah, I cry at zombie movies."

When did Tristan cry? At absurd moments he could never prepare for, maudlin television commercials, movies with lost space aliens, when seeing maimed children or a mistreated pet. At a Lamplighters production of *The Pirates of Penzance,* he was a blubbering mess during an a cappella moment that began "Hail, poetry!" What he thought of at these times was *regret.* One of the lessons of being a grown-up was that life wasn't fair. But every day that Tristan kept living, the unfairness enraged him more and more.

The air was moist. In the dark, the rhythmic spitting of the sprinklers was the sound of civilization. "God, grass," Tristan said. "It just seems weird to be putting grass in where there ought to be sand." He wrinkled his nose at Mik, who would be sure to agree with him. After all, he cared about the environment and treading lightly and living simply and all that. Surely he'd look askance at wasting water.

But Mik shrugged. "It's not like Phoenix—nobody's making lawns around here. If you're going to change an ecosystem, you might as well do it in a graveyard." Tristan was puzzled by that.

The headstone was simple: Joseph I. Jimenez, 1962-1993. Everything else, however, was complicated: the brittle bush, the rose mallow, baskets of flowers. To tell the truth, the garden shocked Tristan the way the comet had—all this attention, so quietly maintained out here in a necropolis. This, like Hale-Bopp, should be on the evening news.

He also felt inadequate. Once a year he sent his twenty-dollar check, and then considered his duty done. But hadn't Joe been the love of his life? Where was his own memorial garden? Did Mrs. Jimenez—and the others—resent Tristan's lax memorializing?

As if he read Tristan's mind, Mik said, "Have you made one of those quilt panels for him?" It wasn't the first time he'd asked. In the past, his "no" had always been sheepish, retiring.

Now he felt defensive and scornful. "Oh, quilt panel, shmilt panel. Leave it to a bunch of fags to come up with something as weepy and cumbersome as a quilt. Good God, I just can't stand it anymore. Why couldn't they think of something a little more sensible, and mobile. Like decorated ice cream sticks?"

Mik and Maria didn't think this was funny. He could see their frowns in the flashlight beam. The cicadas chirped. The sprinklers suddenly went into a triple-time cadence, the sound of a hasty retreat or a return to the beginning of a cycle. They could hear cars on the freeway. He said, "I'm sorry. You see, every week I'm asked to make a quilt panel for somebody. It's too overwhelming. And I'm just not that femmy kind of homo—I can't arrange flowers, I can't dress myself, and I'm sorry, I can't sew."

"I could help you," said Maria.

"I've got some ideas," Mik said.

"Great. That would be great," said Tristan. There was an apologetic silence. Then Tristan said, "I'm sorry if that came off as callous. We all have different ways to grieve, don't we? Somebody once told me that Vietnam vets would get furious when the Vietnamese would smile over body bags. They didn't understand that smiling over the dead was part of their traditional mourning."

Everybody was distracted by this lush place. The grass was soft and manicured and Tristan reclined in it. In the distance, they could hear the calmer rhythmic tchersh-tchersh-tchersh of the sprinklers. In contrast to the marvelous garden of Joe's grave was the proper austerity of Mr. Jimenez's. Mr. Jimenez had died a long time ago, when Joe was eight or nine. Joe always seemed unaffected by his father's death, as far as Tristan could tell. And Maria and Mrs. Jimenez didn't seem terribly altered either.

Above them: the comet. Tristan just loved it.

They were suddenly tired and they all wanted to go home. Maria's trucker husband would be at the end of his rope with the two kids, and there was still her car to fetch. When they dropped him off at the Jimenez B and B, she said, "Be ready tomorrow afternoon at five sharp; I'll pick you up for the Crucifixion at the Easter Ceremonies." They both waved. Mik's car rumbled off into the desert night.

Tristan just stood there. He felt adrift, unfocused. Wasn't this trip supposed to have an itinerary, a route? The visit to the grave seemed uncrucial, or somehow a failure. Perhaps the comet had led them astray. In the morning, it would be invisible, and, Tristan was sure, he would be back on track.

Emptying his pockets onto the dresser before turning in, he took account: change, a pen, a roll of breath mints, his boarding pass stub, and the little notebook. This he'd brought along for his observations of religious heterodoxy and deal making. But all he'd written in the notebook so far was a meaningless list: white Christmas *La Chupapinga* baking bread taxes deep blue sea french fries Debbie Joe.

7

A panda walks into a bar and orders a ham sandwich. The bartender makes the sandwich and puts it in front of the panda. The panda gobbles it down, cinches up his belt, and turns toward the door. Just before he walks out, he turns around, pulls out a six-shooter and aims at the mirror behind the bar, blowing it away in one shot. "Hey," yells the bartender, "what's the big idea?" "I'm a panda," says the panda. "Look it up." And the panda leaves. The bartender gets out a dictionary and finds the definition for "panda." It reads, "Panda, noun. A large black and white mammal of Western China, eats shoots and leaves."

Eight years ago, when she was pregnant with her first kid, Maria had asked—announced—that she was coming up to see Joe and Tristan, and did she need to rent a hotel room or could she stay with them? She was coming alone, which, with twenty-twenty hindsight, Tristan and Joe later realized was an early warning sign of the end of Maria's first marriage. What had thrown them both off the scent was that she was several months pregnant and neverendingly cheerful. Her letter providing the flight number and arrival time was riddled with exclamation points, and the exclamation points had five-point stars where the dots should be.

Despite all the tension of the situation, Tristan liked having out-of-town guests in San Francisco. But Joe wasn't happy with her coming. He'd just been diagnosed and they had scrambled to hide from his family all the evidence of his terrible two-month bout with meningitis.

Tristan remembered how easy it was to lie when Joe's mother called. "He's not here right now, Mrs. Jimenez. He's out on a job site."

"On a Sunday?"

"You know Joe."

Now Maria was coming and of course she couldn't stay in a hotel. They had to find hidey holes for all Joe's meds. He made arrangements to have his infusions at the hospital rather than at home, and they turned down the answering machine in case some blabbermouth doctor started reciting blood workup numbers while they were both out and she was drinking coffee alone in the breakfast nook.

Add to this the smallness of their home: they lived in a charming rustic carriage house with a bedroom that was really an old hayloft. A second room could be approximated, for privacy, by pulling a heavy gold theater curtain across the place where Tristan shelved his books.

Maria wasn't into privacy. Her first night with them, she didn't bother drawing the curtain and uncomplainingly slept in a down mummy sleeping bag on the floor with no padding, despite the hardwood floors, despite the pregnancy.

That morning, Tristan came downstairs to make breakfast and coffee and he could see her across the room, curled in the sack like a question mark. He knew he'd have to tiptoe so he wouldn't wake her. He took the coffee bean grinder out into the garden on one of Joe's heavy orange industrial extension cords in order to keep it quiet.

She came trotting through the back gate just as the ground beans came to rest at the bottom of the Krups—that sleeping bag had been empty. Why did a sleeping bag always look like a body?

"What a gorgeous day," she said.

"Coffee?"

"No, thanks."

"Against your religion?" Maria had just announced that she'd joined a Pentecostal church, and this had also been a cause for concern. So far, she'd kept it to herself, but they wondered when she'd break down and start judging.

Joe was shaking his head a lot throughout the visit. He'd always thought his sister was a repressed lesbian. She'd played a mean game of softball in high school. And now this, this! Born-again amens.

And throughout his illness, they returned again and again to that mystery of Maria's secret fanaticism. It was like a too-tough crossword puzzle. She never once condemned their sinful gayness. She told Joe that she was praying for him, although not to cure him of homosexuality, but AIDS. Once, she let slip that she was volunteering for Operation Rescue, saving the unborn from abortions, but after she'd told that to Tristan and Joe in an almost boastful voice, she had clammed up, embarrassed. It was as if she pulled another version of herself out of a drawer for her brother and his lover. "Probably," Joe once mused, "she just figures we're going to hell, and there's no need for her to punish us here on earth."

But even in that first bloom of born-again zeal, she seemed balanced. Coffee probably was against her religion, but she said, "No, I just heard about your coffee."

And so he made her a special cup of weak coffee. Just to see what she would do. She looked at it and pointed at her pregnant belly. Was there any part of her that really *was* Pentecostal, besides the act of conversion? Perhaps, Tristan theorized with Joe, Maria just wanted to find some way of distinguishing herself from other members of her family: it was something she could have for herself, a room of her own.

Joe shrugged. "In any case, don't be surprised if one day she doesn't lash out at us or turn us in to the God Squad."

Tristan didn't believe she'd ever do that. Nevertheless, Tristan did not respect it. Swapping Catholicism for Pentecostalism seemed vulgar, like choosing a sofa-sized landscape painting over a Van Gogh.

And that afternoon, after she refused the coffee and Joe dragged his sorry ass out of bed, they all went over to Oakland in Thumper, Joe's big white van, to hit the Pick-Your-Part auto graveyard. He could get good deals on parts by stripping them off old cars and buying them by the pound.

When they arrived at the open field of junked cars, Joe quickly disappeared in search of a certain-sized carburetor, and left Tristan and Maria alone together.

Tristan found a broken-off radio antenna and he was playing with it as if he were a fairy with a wand. The Latino dudes in the checkout shack at the gates were watching him like a hawk. Or maybe they were staring at Maria, pretty even with her slightly pooched-out belly.

Maria was inspecting the trunks of the cars, looking for abandoned things. "This is great," she said, "Like the way flea markets used to be."

Good, there was something they could agree on. "No kidding," said Tristan, "people sell Coca-Cola bottles like they used to sell silvered mirrors. There aren't any bargains any more."

"Joe can spot 'em," she said. She found a doll head lodged in the well where a spare tire was supposed to be. "I suppose we ought to help him, but I don't even know where to look for a carburetor."

"Me either." Wow, they were bonding like crazy. "I don't have a mechanical mind." Tristan suddenly felt tired, like he'd been tiptoeing since he saw the sleeping bag that morning. Joe had begged him—nicely—not to swear if he could help it. He didn't know whether Maria would take offense.

"So when are you due?" he asked, tapping her belly with his antenna-wand.

"Oh, not until November. I get to carry this kid all the way through an Arizona summer, yee-hah!" She'd turned to examining the little identifying insignia of cars, classic and not: "Astre," "Bonneville," "Grand Prix." "Joe used to have an old beater van in Tucson, a Chevrolet. He scraped off all the letters so that it just spelled 'C-V-O-T, C-vot.' He said it stood for 'Cruise Vehicle of Tomorrow.'"

"I don't know why he calls Thumper Thumper. He won't tell me."

"Joe likes to have secrets. He's so skinny! Are you guys getting enough to eat? And why is he avoiding me?"

Tristan nearly stepped in a big puddle of oil, like some concentrated dose of badness pooled at his feet. Maria had come across a big Ford truck, resting on its axles, and leaned against it, so that there were little flakes of rust on her elbows when she stood up straight again. Before he could even begin to feel guilty about withholding information from her, she was on to other subjects. "I just love being pregnant, hot weather or not. Do you think you'll ever have kids?"

Women always asked him that question. How could he explain that he had no interest at all, without sounding selfish? "I'm afraid I'd screw it up," he said. "If I had had a kid at the age when my dad had me, my kid would be in junior high by now. I'd have to be a scoutmaster or something."

"You'd figure it out."

Tristan shook his head. "Too many emergencies. When I was an infant, my dad picked me up by the arms and accidentally pulled them out of their sockets."

"Oooh!" She winced. "Did it hurt?"

"I don't remember; I was too little. They took me to the emergency room and the doctor just popped them back into place. Pop!" Maria was holding her belly but probably not thinking about the fact that she was holding her belly. "I used to tease my dad about that when I grew up, but he didn't think it was funny at all. It made him very sad."

"Can you imagine explaining it nowadays? They'd have you taken away from him, for child abuse or something. Do you think it made you gay?"

Tristan laughed. "Opera made me gay."

"You like opera? Can you take me to an opera while I'm visiting?"

"Sorry, the season is over." If Maria were in an opera, what would it be? Light opera, one of those Strauss operations, or one where they sing about champagne and a couple of borzois are trotted out on stage.

"What do you guys do for fun?" She'd returned her attention to the "Ford" symbol on the truck, polished it with a hanky she'd pulled out of nowhere.

What did they do? Pleasure: sex, food, music, travel. Whatever felt good. He supposed they were selfish, but hell, Joe was dying. "We tell each other jokes. I know a joke; do you want to hear it?"

"Uh-oh," she said. She'd pulled an emery board out of nowhere, too, and was wedging it between the door panel and the little symbol. "Go ahead."

"No, really, it's funny. And clean. I swear. It's funny, I think, because it's clean. Somebody told it to me and you know, I live in San Francisco, where everybody is trying to be the most transgressive. People walking around naked, etcetera, with bird cages on their heads. I saw a porno movie in the video store yesterday called *Japanese Sewer Sluts*."

Joe came from around the corner. He'd made quite a haul. Two carburetors and a long, thin rearview mirror, one that they would use for the rest of his life to slip into Joe's mouth to check the spread of Kaposi's sarcoma lesions on the roof of his mouth. Joe had a double-jointed jaw or something, and could fit the whole thing in. It was a sight.

Tristan recalled that moment: while Joe showed them his prizes, Maria had not looked at the carburetors but at a huge unsightly wart on Joe's hand that had been burned off twice and come back again. She looked from the wart to Tristan and the look referred to her unanswered question she'd let drop: "Why is he avoiding me?" The look, indescribable, was one he'd always remembered. She knew, and though she never said she did when it all came out, the way he'd looked back at her at that moment said, "Yes, you're right." This, Tristan always believed, was what made them so close.

"I was just getting ready to tell Maria a joke. Have you heard my clean joke about the panda?" Tristan said, making sure Joe heard him say it was clean. He told the joke, which he really did love. It had a kind of literary punch to it, and he planned on telling it to his students in class one day.

Maria said, "Oh sure, I know that joke. Only I heard it differently. I heard it was the panda going to see a whore, and he goes down on her and she really loves it, him eating her out like that —" Joe and Tristan stared at each other as if she'd just lifted her blouse— "and he suddenly gets up, puts on his hat, and leaves, and she says, 'Hey, what's the big idea?' And the panda says, 'I'm a panda. Look it up.' So she gets out the dictionary and she sees 'Panda: a large black and white mammal of Western China, eats bush and leaves."

She pried off the "Ford" logo and pocketed it, and when they went to weigh and pay for all the parts they'd picked, she never showed it to the Latino guys who'd been staring at her.

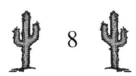 8

After breakfast, Tristan headed for downtown Tucson. While leaving the adobe, Tristan noticed for the first time, here in broad daylight, that Mrs. Jimenez had painted her bed-and-breakfast place red and green. It was a big garish Christmas decoration.

Later, when he teasingly made a remark about it, Mrs. Jimenez would say, "Well, it's hard to tell, isn't it, what something's going to look like before you actually do it? Those boys at the hardware store warned me that colors always dry a shade darker than when they go on wet, but did I listen? Then again, think of it like a broken clock. Once a year, it tells the right time!" Actually, thought Tristan, a broken clock told the right time 730 times a year, but why cause trouble? This was funny until he later heard Maria say the same thing, and realized it was something Mrs. Jimenez said to all her guests.

On the town, Tristan drank coffee, which he loved, in a café where he overheard nobody, refreshingly, talking about their personal feelings or development. He watched a pack of college students honking their horns down the street: the university's basketball team was in the Final Four and on every corner, T-shirts were for sale. He browsed at a bookstore where he bought a little booklet on the details of the Yaqui Easter, and found a book about holy places in Sonora, so he bought that, too.

It looked like it might rain. There were immensely tall thunderheads in every direction that looked like the shapes of Midwestern states. He rushed back to the adobe and waited in the garden for the storm to come. Living in San Francisco, he rarely got to enjoy a good thunderstorm. But no matter how dark it got, no matter the rumblings and heat lightning and even gray streaks in the distance that he assumed was rain, not a drop fell on him in his folding chair among the poppies. Mrs. Jimenez came out to put up her big thirsty hotel towels on the line.

She was in her gardening outfit, a black and white horizontal-striped mock turtleneck with a pair of black denim overalls. She looked like a squat mime.

While he read, she dithered in the garden for a few minutes and then he could see her relief: she spotted the wooden swing, an unfinished project. "I hired a Mexican guy to stain it," she lamented to Tristan. "And he claimed he'd done staining before. Or maybe that's what I understood. I keep forgetting the limits of my Spanish. In any case, he's done a terrible job and I'm going to have to do it again, myself."

"Aren't you afraid it's going to rain on you?" he asked when it was apparent that she was going to paint the swing right now. He pointed up at the purple storm clouds.

"They call it *verga* in Spanish," she said. "It's when the rain evaporates in the hot dry air before it hits the ground."

He read silently, looking up now and then to watch her work. He could tell she wanted to have a conversation with him, but was trying to find a way of getting at it. Finally:

"Have you been reading all the stuff about these protease inhibitors?"

Tristan smiled. That was it. "Of course. Everybody is hoping. It's a wonder, you know? The obituary section in the San Francisco paper is getting smaller and smaller. Just last week, there were only three of them—and one was from natural causes."

Mrs. Jimenez put the rag down and clapped her hands together with joy, but it was the practiced gesture of an innkeeping hostess. Then she went back to work, thinking.

"Of course, there are still a few friends," Tristan said, "who may be too late. You know, their immune systems are too far gone. They watch the rest as if they've missed a train and they're standing on a platform. . . . " He could see that she was just staring at the cardboard she'd torn up from a refrigerator box to catch the stain drips.

"Yes, missed the train," she said.

He stood up and walked over, squatted down to her level. Thank God she wasn't crying. "I know. I know how you feel. I feel the same way."

It was only a partial lie. He did know this feeling, but it was neck and neck with the gloriously selfish feeling that he'd outlived Joe, and every day won the race by an even wider margin. When he had that other, nasty feeling, it surged, like a bloodlust, and he responded to it by saying "Wow!" to himself. He'd sort it out later. "How can we not feel jealous at the lucky ones? It's just luck, you know, good, bad timing."

"I walk by houses in the evening," Mrs. Jimenez said, "and I watch people sit in front of their televisions. I look over in this parking lot and watch the *borrachos* beg for a can of beer. And I have nothing but contempt. How can you waste your life? I want to shake them. How can you ruin it, ruin your health? You bastards, I hate you all." She waited a beat and Tristan strained his ears, as if listening for the lowest note just outside the range of human hearing, feeling a throb in his eustachian tubes. And then Mrs. Jimenez grinned. "And then I go straight to confession and do whatever penance I'm given, twice, just for thinking such terrible thoughts."

"Yes," Tristan said. He'd felt that too.

"I get all the pamphlets now, you know," she said. "I got on the mailing lists once Joe started getting sick—GMHC news, that one especially. I never bothered getting off the lists. 'Please Remove,' that's what you write. Then they know what's happened. I didn't want them to know. I wanted them to think all that mailing worked. I get notices about doing studies. Donation envelopes. I'm an expert now!"

Tristan recalled her initial response to Joe's illness—week after week, she'd pay for masses at her church. When Joe found out, he was enraged. He was the one who got her on all those mailing lists.

"I know all the names and numbers—sequinivir, nelfinivir, crixovan. Don't they sound like drag queen names?" she giggled. She'd been saving that one for Tristan, he could tell. "Why don't you boys get together and dress up as the protease sisters?" She kept pronouncing it pro-teez, but Tristan didn't correct her, afraid it might ruin her joke, and then she might cry after all. Humor, he thought pedantically, is like *verga.*

"What good is being an expert now?" She tugged Tristan's sleeve as a kind of tender gesture.

Tristan smiled. "Whenever I go on a trip to Europe, Mexico, whatever, I never read the guidebook until I come back home. I say, 'Oh, that was what that was,' and, 'Hey, I've been there.' "

"I'm just the same way," Mrs. Jimenez said. "It's perverse, isn't it?"

Murphy came skittering out, stepped in a puddle of stain, and apparently ate a clod of dirt. "Grubs," Mrs. Jimenez explained. "What he probably lived on when he was out in the desert."

Tristan considered the fact of Murphy as some kind of ascetic hermit in the wilderness, in a small cabin of clay and wattles made.

When he leaned over to pet Murphy, he tipped over a glass of ice tea and it smashed on the concrete. "Oh jeez," he apologized all over the place, "I'm such a clod. And near the pool, too; that's really bad."

"You sit right there; you've got bare feet," said Mrs. Jimenez. "I'll bring out the Dustbuster." The cleanup set her in motion again. After clearing the shards, she continued on her orderly way, the conversation closed, for now.

Under the *verga,* Tristan read about the Yaqui. "The Yaqui believe that Jesus should be represented as a very old man, and the name *viejito,* 'little old man,' is a term of respect. A member of the group of masked tricksters, the Chapayekas, reluctantly sits before the cross in front of the church while he is crowned with cottonwood leaves and rope made of horsehair. He then trudges in fatigue from cross to cross in the stations, and the other Chapayekas mock him with imaginary food and water. He then asks money from the crowd." Tristan would have to remember to bring some cash to give the *viejito.*

For years, Tristan had been, ironically, a poor example of charitable giving. After all, what was he saving it for? But he saw charity as an investment of sorts, a way of being selfish. Why give, when there was no tomorrow? Now he watched himself write checks in large amounts to the most ridiculous of charities.

He went in to see where Mrs. Jimenez was, but she must have stepped out. He called out in the room, but nobody answered. On top of her television was her favorite picture of Joe and Tristan together riding two horses, from the year they'd spent Thanksgiving at a dude ranch in Utah. That was the Thanksgiving before Joe's first big fall, from the meningitis. But when they were on the horses, everything was perfect. Life with Joe in those years was like experiencing decadent Roman orgies every day. Every day that dinner-table question was posed: If you knew you were going to die tomorrow, what would you do? And every day, they did it. They'd eaten so much at that bunkhouse Thanksgiving feast, they each stepped out of the cabin in the night and decadently forced themselves to vomit. In the morning, the magical mule deer had eaten all of the evidence. Look how innocent we look, Tristan thought: neither of us was even thinking about the Turn of the Century.

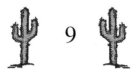

9

"You don't think you're as bald as you are, do you?" Maria said as she smeared sunblock over Tristan's face and forehead. "If you don't put some up here"—she dabbed amazingly high up on his crown—"and here, you're going to be one sorry sight." She leaned back on her heels to get a look at her work, as if she'd just done a beauty makeover. "I'm sorry, Tristan. Is that a sensitive issue for you?"

On the contrary, Tristan had been astonished, in the last two years, at the phenomenon of growing old. He'd peer into a bathroom mirror and look at the crow's-feet around his eyes. When the barber cut his hair he fought the urge to collect the shiny silver hairs, like minnows flashing in a bait bucket. And that he didn't notice his receding hairline reflected more a disbelief in his age than in the actual loss. So close to the border now, should he make a pharmacy run to Nogales for miracle cures? Retin-A? minoxidil?

Maria said, "You got to watch yourself out there. I know it's getting close to sunset, but you'll still be out in it for two or three hours, and you don't want to get fried on the first day." Was it his imagination, or was she slapping his forehead, rather than applying the block? She seemed a little more impatient with him, too. "We've gotta go. You don't want to miss the Crucifixion."

Tristan wasn't sure he was up to this—three straight days of traditional Yaqui Easter ritual.

"What if they don't like me?" He'd read all the cautions in the pamphlet about not taking pictures of the ceremonies, not being obtrusive. "I mean, you can pass, but I'm pretty white."

"Yes, and big. I'm expecting you to protect me if there's any trouble. Oh, Tristan, nobody's going to bug us as long as we don't take pictures or notes."

"Notes?" Not even notes? "What if they stop everything and see me and say, 'Get the white guy out of here'?"

She shook her head. "It's not like that. Get in the truck. Mik's already waiting for us at the rez."

They had to stop along the way at a McDonald's Drive-Thru because Mik was playing the Monopoly game, and, being a Muslim, and also a vegetarian, the only thing he could eat there was the french fries. "Do you want anything?" she asked Tristan.

He shook his head. He'd been learning how to be mean to his body again—martinis, not enough sleep, skipping a week at the gym—but he couldn't bring himself back to fast food, not just yet.

Maria ordered a combo meal and opened the game piece herself. "Pennsylvania Avenue. I don't think he's got that one."

When she parked by an overpass, they could see Mik waiting on the curb. "Hey, Monkey!" Maria yelled to get his attention. "Pennsylvania Avenue? Have you got that one?"

Mik shook his head excitedly. "No, and that may be a winner. I wish I had my game board with me."

"Is this going to ruin our fun?"

"I can wait," said Mik. Tristan wondered, was it a compliment or prejudice to say that Muslims were stoic?

They walked across the overpass, and they were there.

"This is it?" Tristan asked. "This is the reservation?"

"This is it!" said Maria.

The Yaqui village was situated all along the side of the freeway overpass. Endless streams of cars and trucks roared unromantically over them. The Yaqui church, a cinder block structure painted white and adorned with two bell towers, strung with hundreds of napkin flowers, abutted an on-ramp. Tristan thought: still screwing the Indians.

Above it all rose a glittery billboard advertising the reservation's casino complex down the road: "Loosest Slots!" and a rolling jackpot figure, then freeway directions.

They walked through the dust. Chickens were stalking about, and an old lady was feeding them marigold petals to attain that desired yellow color when the time came for them to be plucked and cooked. Jaundice, Tristan thought, is a virtue. Somebody was selling hand-cranked ice cream in unlikely flavors like *arroz*-and-*queso* and the more poetic, but alarmingly unrevealing, *"beso de ángel."* There were a few slinky sore-covered dogs with winsome, wise, and patient expressions. Tristan thought about Joe, in those last days.

In the parking lot, a huge crowd watched the ceremonial Crucifixion. Tristan was disoriented when he saw the crucifix go up into the air. They'd selected a very skinny statue for their Christ. He looked dead already.

"They call him *El Viejo*," Maria said, "the old one. They like to think he was an old man who comes back as the baby Jesus." This was no clownish Chapayeka pretending to be *viejito*—it was the real thing. For some reason, Tristan felt betrayed. By whom? The Yaquis? The pamphlet?

The statue of *El Viejo* had a gruesome face of pain and suffering. The whole world exists, Tristan let himself enunciate, in the moment before the Savior reigns, in torture. "By your suffering I am comforted in my own suffering."

It was something about the way the cross swooped smoothly up in a smooth arc, and popped into place.

Tristan surprised himself by crying. Mik grabbed him by the arm. "Let's go get salditos," he said, and trotted Tristan in the opposite direction of the Crucifixion. Maria stayed to watch. Mik distracted Tristan. Tristan let him.

Mik said, "He suffered a ton, didn't he?"

Several times that question had been put to Tristan, and he denied like Peter before the crowing of the cock. This far away, this time, Tristan said, "God, Mik, you wouldn't think a human was capable of that kind of thing. Jesus put up with it for a few hours. Imagine being crucified for months. And then it doesn't even redeem the world! I was—I was mad at him for it. His body could just take it and take it."

In work, in sickness, even in sex, Joe never cried out. He had a bizarre high threshold for pain that may have hastened his death, Tristan sometimes decided. He'd go too far before resting his body.

Mik said, "If you had called, I would have come."

"I know. But that's just the thing. Even our friends down the street would say, 'Anything we can do?' And other than making a casserole or running an errand, there really wasn't anything. I would never call his mother because I was afraid I'd have to take care of both of them."

Mik nodded. But his reply, Tristan thought, was incongruous: "But he died anyway."

It was their turn in line. The concessions vendor was selling lard in all its forms. Refried beans, bean burros, Cokes. Mik said, "Give us two salditos and a lime."

He gave the lady fifty cents and she handed him two shriveled brown nuggets. Mik handed one to Tristan. "They're bitter plums, cured in salt. Take half of this lime"— he was cutting it open with the pocket knife (the one Tristan had given him; in just a day it had been used one hundred percent more often than it had been in the last four years)— "and suck on it. Keeps your body supplied with salt out in the sun."

Tristan dared a taste. It was horrific, not even a hint of a plum's good sweetness. "This is vile!" he enthused. It was like something ACT UP would endorse as an alternative therapy.

Mik slapped him on the back. "I know! You'll get used to it." They went back over to the parking lot Crucifixion. Two fat little Yaqui girls were skipping rope. A guy was selling small neon glow-wands in blues and greens and reds. They drew mosquito hawks in the twilight.

"Hey, Monkey!" Maria yelled for their attention. The whole place was dusty. Tristan knew this smell: fry bread, smoke, dust, dogs, fish. He'd been in Alaska and smelled it, and in Havasupai Canyon; it was a reservation smell.

Everybody had come home for the holidays. Mik told him he'd been driving by the village after work every night this week and saw men raking the sand in the plaza, refurbishing the church, building a giant effigy of Judas, which stood at the far end of the plaza, laced with firecrackers. The promise of flames could keep a crowd waiting for days.

"God, it's wide open," Tristan said of the church, for the entire side facing the plaza was exposed like a garage big enough for two or three semis to back into.

"They built it just for this ceremony," Mik told him. "The rest of the year it's kept shut, but when you see how often they come running in and out of there, you'll understand why it needs to be wide open." There were flowers everywhere. Over the ramada. Hung from rafters on the inside. At the side was a huge mound of petals of many different kinds of flowers, like an industrial sachet of potpourri for the gods.

Tristan thought of Mrs. Jimenez's house in green and red, also relevant one day of the year.

Mik put his two hands up in a frame of fingers, L and 7, the symbol usually used to say somebody was square. "But it's still a Golden Section," he said. "That perfect design you'll find in the Parthenon or any well-designed building."

"Look." Maria tugged on Tristan's pantleg. "The Fariseos." Dozens of men had come drifting out from behind the church, the Pharisees, the ones who persecuted Jesus. They were evil incarnate; the officers carried wooden swords, or flags with green crosses. They were in hot black pants, shirts, and capes trimmed with purple, and wore black fedoras even when they went into the church.

"They've made a vow to play the role of the bad guy," Mik explained. He was the great explainer. "They understand that without evil there can be no good, and this ritual playacting is all for the greater glory of God."

The Maestros, leaders of the church group and organizers of the ceremony, dressed in Sunday-go-to-meeting clothes, with no formal insignia, men, women, and children, were making a chant, the song version of a tuneless whistle. Behind them were the foot soldiers, the Chapayekas, who mulled around mimicking the Maestros, making noises with the sets of rattles wrapped around their bellies. They congregated around the big Judas effigy, for he was their saint. They had papier maché heads in ghoulish Native American designs, white with short horns and big ears, but also, goofy designs of policemen, cartoon characters, animals, a China-man with a Fu Manchu and a negro with immense lips. Nobody minded that the Yaqui made blackface, Tristan thought. Perhaps brutal poverty exempted sensitivity of every sort.

The Chapayekas were the clowns and tricksters of this drama. Tristan thought of Wagner's operas again, about the trickster god Loki, out to obey only Wotan, and then just maybe. If the officers of the Fariseos were overdressed here in the desert with their black clothing, the Chapayekas must have been dying. Besides the full face masks, they wore heavy rugs over clothes, bound with the deer-hoof rattles.

Mik wrinkled his brow. "I want you to meet somebody." He reached out and grabbed a boy and turned him around in his grip. "This is Refugio," he said. "A Matachini."

Tristan had read about the Matachini. The word had caught his eye like all secret sexual words, titillating even after years of permissive life. After all, the Matachine Society had been the first gay organization in the country, a masonic-like political organiza-tion that took its name from medieval court jesters. No doubt, so had the Yaqui ceremony—for it was an all-male society in the ceremony that wore dresses in honor of their matron, the Virgin Mary. And not just dresses—flamboyant outfits festooned with ribbons and sashes. They wore embroidered blouses. They wore headresses of colorful crepe paper strips.

Mik said, "Refugio, this is Tristan." Had Tristan been staring?

But with so much going on around him, the boy had to let his eyes and concentration swivel into focus. When he did, he said, "You are sunburned." Tristan was glad Refugio said this instead of something about his being bald or white. Any minute now, they were going to ask him to leave.

"Tristan knew Joe," Mik explained.

Refugio lit up. Tristan realized this boy was barely thirteen. He was fat in an overeating kind of way. The kind of fat that kids picked on until one autumn the fat boy returned to school trans-formed into the studliest lady-killer of them all. Tristan felt the urge to pull Refugio aside to tell him this. Refugio said, "What was it like?"

Tristan looked to Mik.

Mik said, "Refugio is gay. He told me this and I told him about Joe and how he did okay being gay."

Tristan wondered at this, how this boy would confess a thing like that to Mik—how did they know each other? And he also wondered if Joe being dead precluded his being "okay." Mik told the boy that Tristan was gay, too. "And do you see how he's okay, too?"

Refugio smiled. Tristan smiled back but shook his head. "Kids these days," he said. "How do you know you're gay at such an age? It took me years to figure it out."

Refugio shrugged. A few tassels of his Matachini hat bobbled. "I just know."

Before any of them realized what was going on, five of the Chapayekas had surrounded Maria and separated her from Mik and Tristan. Village girls, with their hair let down for the occasion, giggled as the Chapayekas pantomimed hunting Maria, perhaps recognized as the Mudflap Girl of Their Dreams, like a rabbit. They gently bounced her around and made the rattles around their bellies roll in unison.

"*Conejo, conejo,*" the locals close to the Chapayekas muttered. They did a rhythmic stomping around her. Maria was amused. She obliged them by hopping around like the rabbit they were calling her. She even did a rabbity nose wrinkle.

Tristan felt concern, but Mik was calm, still observant, and that made Tristan calm, too. Mik said, "See how they stab her with their knives in the left hand only? They always do things left-handed, or backward."

The Chapayekas merrily bounced Maria like a pinball in their circle. Maria was being a good sport about it. Then, as if they had it all planned out, they hoisted her up over their heads like a trophy. She made a beautiful captive.

"What do you make of all this?" Tristan asked Mik. "I mean, as a non-Christian."

Mik shrugged. "I think we can all agree that suffering has been the inspiration for a lot of beautiful art."

Ah-ha, redemption, Tristan thought. How Christian of you. Hopeful. "Have you seen it before?"

"Some of it. You can't really see the whole thing. You have to sleep some time. It's boring for hours, and then suddenly everything happens."

Like Wagner.

"You know I love the artifice," Mik smiled. He was referring to the first time Joe had brought Tristan down to meet his family, and Tristan had tacitly understood—misunderstood—that Mik was also gay. Mik had accompanied the two of them (led them, really) down to Nogales. Tristan remembered that whole weekend very well.

The Chapayekas weren't through with Maria. They'd started jumping up and down with her, and watching her body jerk around reminded Tristan of a car wreck. All this physical exertion—in *that* many clothes—in *this* kind of heat—he thought, these guys must be *on* something. Jacked up on goofballs, as Joe used to say. Refugio and a couple of the other Matachinis (not apparently gay, but gaily dressed anyway) were dancing around the outskirts, egging them on.

Then he heard Maria say, "Hey, help me. Somebody please help." It was quiet but sincere, and that's what made it so urgent.

The Chapayekas weren't backing off. Her cries made them get even more rough. They kicked up dust. They were moving to the big pile of flower petals. Did they imagine that this would be enough cushion to throw her into? She would be black and blue if they thought that was enough for a soft landing. Tristan ran through a hundred possibilities, all of them violent. He felt helpless. There seemed to be no formal rules about honoring the fourth wall of theater, the place from where the audience classically observed but did not participate. This was modern theater and audience participation (or abduction) was expected. Nevertheless, Tristan, as a white man, had no business to intervene. Mik was still standing in his studious position, always that damn outsider.

"What should we do?" Tristan asked Refugio.

"About what?" said Refugio. Tristan noticed that Refugio had decorated his hat with feather duster feathers and the kind of lick-on stars that teachers give out for good grades.

"They're going to hurt her." He could clearly see that she was crying now, struggling, which only made them handle her more roughly. They were making mocking sounds. Some boys not in costume also squealed, "Help, help."

"They're only doing this to impersonate evil," said Mik. "They've made a vow to Jesus."

The Chapayekas were paying attention to some sort of pattern, even in the ugly movement that molestation makes.

"Oye, conejito," some kid yelled.

The world, thought Tristan, was full of suffering. Was Mik thinking it always bred beautiful images?

Simultaneously, they lowered her to the hard-packed earth and pushed her with their long sticks. One, dressed like a hobo with an old ratty wool coat ("houndstooth," Tristan identified), directed them to trap her with their wooden scabbards. A man in the crowd laughed, and, testing impromptu authority, gave a command in something that wasn't Spanish or English that meant, get on top of her, Smear-the-Queer style. They were about to do just that, when a cry from the ramada of the church brought their attention back to the ceremony.

Suddenly they heard pretty, melodious bells and ankle rattles, and shrill flutes. A drum. The Pascola dancers, in masks and with their hair in topknots, were telling jokes, and the Chapayekas wanted to hear them. They ran off as if they'd been rumbling or assaulting and a squad car had pulled up.

Maria lay, inert, on the ground, two perfect tear streaks sliding down her dusty face. Her body shuddered in a sob, and Tristan thought it looked like an orgasm, or a body in a seat on a plane that had to land on a too-short runway. He ran over to her.

"Are you okay? Hey, Maria? It's over."

She wouldn't look at him, she was something like ashamed. "Just get me the hell out of here," she yelled. Three old Yaqui ladies laughed, which meant, oh, quit overreacting, girlie, if you're going to run around looking like the Mudflap Girl, what do you expect?

"Hey, Monkey," said Mik, who had just sauntered up.

Refugio was beside him. "You are a beautiful little rabbit," he said.

"Shut the hell up," she said.

Suddenly, from behind, some kids let off a string of firecrackers that made them jump. Out ran ten pudgy Yaqui boys in skirts. Maria began to bawl.

10

That time when Joe was still alive and they went down to Nogales, Mik had been driving, so Joe and Tristan could get wasted on margaritas. Joe said he befriended his Muslim buddy so he'd always have a Designated Driver.

They'd come on business, first and foremost: to get a couple of experimental drugs for Joe, as yet unavailable in the States. One was an antifungal, another was some sort of skin irritant said to stimulate the immune system. Plus they were going to a pharmacist known to stock a good deal of AZT, so they'd brought a lot of cash with them in case they needed anything else. The *farmacias* were a treasure trove of items like penicillin and cootie lotions and impossibly powerful headache remedies. Quack cures mixed in. The recommended pharmacist gave them the hard sell, and wanted to sell them more than they wanted to carry with them. Joe was firm, though, and got just what he had come for, along with a big box, factory sealed and labeled zidovudine, AZT. It cost half of what they expected it to because Joe could haggle in Spanish.

They went to a tavern and did mission-accomplished tequila shots, while Mik drank bottled water. In the plaza outside, gringo tourists could pay for a song from more than a dozen mariachi bands loitering around. Two of the mariachi bands had come into the bar and were competing for the clientele's attention. Tristan leaned over to Mik and said, "I think one mariachi band would be enough."

Mik smiled and said, almost above the din, "In the world."

They were hungry and Joe ordered *menudo con garbanzos.* When it came to the table, Joe made a horrified face and said, "It's tripe; my God, tripe."

Tristan said, "That's what *menudo* is."

"It is not."

"It is."

"Then why didn't you stop me?"

"Because this is your home. I thought maybe you knew something about this place that I didn't."

They were so embarrassed they had to carry it away to another table before abandoning it, so the guys who cooked it couldn't see. There was a drunken argument about whether or not Joe always had to be in charge, always the know-it-all, even when he didn't know it all. Mostly, it was a mockery of an argument.

A man with a box full of wires went table to table, and for a few pesos, you could play a bizarre drinking game involving electricity and trust. The boxkeeper explained that the three of them should hold hands, one with a metal bulb that came from the machine and the one on the end completing the circuit with a second bar. As the man revved up the box, a current ran through them, and whoever pulled away first and broke the circuit would create a shock for everybody. The point, Tristan guessed, was to trust the others. But when the current became too high, he had a terrible vision of his liver burning up inside him. He pulled away. The wet shudder of several volts of electricity seemed to have made him drunker. The other two should have been angry or disappointed in him for letting go, but they seemed to like the pain.

They swilled tequila, and they decided to split up for a few hours since everybody had a different agenda: Joe thought their house needed a new rug and wanted to try his hand at haggling (since he'd been so successful getting a good price for the drugs), Tristan had decided to get a haircut because they only cost four bucks, and Mik wanted to go to the Nogales cemetery because they had a Jewish section. It wasn't Muslim, but it was close enough, he said. It was the monumental joke of the story that this was the part of the day when things started going wrong.

Tristan went down the street and found at least four haircutters. He never understood why businesses of the same type would be grouped together like that. In another street, there was store after store of wedding gowns. He asked a friendly boy, *"¿Dónde está la peluquería más mejor?"* La *peluquería,* the boy wondered, a beauty salon? Tristan was always getting one word wrong.

But the boy corrected him—*"La mejor peluquería está alli"*— and pointed and Tristan went into a barbershop and found himself in a neighborhood hangout. Plenty of other kinds of transactions were going on in the room, nothing illegal, but nothing likely, either. A careworn woman, presumably the barber's wife, was selling roses from a yellow bucket. Two little girls were selling rosaries and holy water.

"Quisiera un corte de pelo," Tristan said and sat down in the chair. The barber got up. He was in a white lab coat, like a doctor. Tristan, made brave by margaritas, decided to have a conversation. Was he the best barber? He had come recommended. This charmed the barber, who rose to the occasion and cut Tristan's hair very short, the way Tristan wanted it, and used all sorts of lotions and tinctures and a real leather strop to sharpen his blades.

Tristan loved the danger of a real razor slicing off the hair on his lower neck. Hair grew there, hair was growing everywhere but on his head these days, out of his nostrils and ears; he had two epaulets of the stuff on each shoulder and knew it would spread in the future. Barbers in San Francisco were too polite to go after unseemly hair, and he had to depend on Joe's gorillalike grooming. This barber, however, had no fear, and didn't even question. He had special instruments to get the ear hair and boldly shave down his back. It all slid down the plastic sheet tied around his neck and onto the floor, where the barber had not bothered to sweep up the cuttings from at least a half-dozen other customers. Spotlessness was not the sign of a good barber here, Tristan guessed, but rather the mounding of all these locks was a testimony to his prowess. It piled like cornhusks or autumn leaves and had the same connotations of pleasant abundance.

The barber chatted with him, sometimes about how he liked his hair length and sometimes introducing the people in the shop—the flower lady was his sister, not his wife—and while Tristan got most of it, sometimes he let a question slide with an emphatic nod, meaning, I understand, which he did not.

So Tristan didn't really realize that the barber had shaven his famously bushy eyebrows clean off, and wouldn't know it until hours later, when he met Mik and Joe at the bullfight ring and they laughed at him.

Under the influence of the same margaritas, Joe had been cheated on an ersatz Navajo rug, and Tristan would have forgiven the cost and the cheap materials had it not been so damn ugly, to boot. He still kept that rug rolled up in the closet in San Francisco. Perhaps that should be Joe's quilt panel?

But the finale of that day came courtesy of Mik, who loved the bullfights and managed to snag three tickets *"de sombra."* Up to that point, Mik had been practically inscrutable to Tristan. But when he watched the Muslim wax ecstatic over the slaughter of half a dozen brave bulls, Tristan forgave Mik his need for animal cruelty. Between all the bullfighting rules he told Joe and Tristan, he apologized.

"I know it seems like carnage, but you have to understand the beauty of the artifice," he said. "If you like opera, Tristan, you'll love this. It's a metaphor for reality."

Joe said, "If it's a metaphor, why do they cut the horses' vocal cords so you can't hear the screaming when the bulls gore them?"

Joe was no moralist. He didn't usually come up with positions like that. He needled Mik about the bullfights only because Mik had fed him the lines himself—something Mik was prone to do. No, Joe was not one to formulate precis on right and wrong, but he did the next best thing: he instinctively attached himself to moral people. Well, nice people.

The bullfights. Yes, they were like opera, because the tickets were so expensive one couldn't be blasé about them. Like opera, the bullfighting was not quite sport, not quite art, not quite natural. It had its long dull passages in preparation for the great performance, that aria, that scene, that Wagnerian moment when the *gesamkunstwerk* really worked.

They piled into the stands with not much room to move around. They'd rented cushions from the Club de Leones to sit on the cement stands. *"Gracias por su donativo,"* they read. The sand in the ring was smoothed and ochre-orange, very particularly. Two concentric rings in red were the only markings. Blood, sun, sand. Those three or four trumpets playing an insolent, swaggering tap, repeated over the course of the three hours every time the picadores came out, or the horsemen. The picadores stepped out from behind protective wooden covers, six of them in all. They all, with the matador, wore the "suits of light," which seemed to Tristan to be good for maybe one bullfight. It appeared to be the point of the thing to get close enough to the bull to get a mess on you; the best matador did.

Then came the bull, angry and bewildered, a single blue ribbon pinned into his back. The picadores lured him with capes of day-glo pink and seams of day-glo yellow. Tristan wondered if these served to madden the bull more, those bright teeny-bopper colors, bubble gum and dandelions.

As at the opera, the crowd demanded of itself total silence. If some *borracho* shouted something stupid, he was removed immediately. The crowd was rather Roman, circus, lots of thumbs up, thumbs down. It seemed to converse with itself, deciding whether the bullfighter performed a good move or not; Tristan got better at discovering what moves were good: the verónica, the half verónica.

Mik called the moves out: a graceful wrap of the cape around the matador's body: *"Chicuelina."* One-handed swirl: *"Rebolera."* The fight was divided up into thirds, the final, Tristan loved, was called "The Third of the Death."

It was about the bull, who must die bravely. If the matador could instill a sense of having something to die bravely for, then he was a success. If a matador could not, then it was he, not the bull, who was jeered.

Nevertheless, allegiances were odd at these bullfights. Even after a death-defying performance, most of the matadors didn't dare come out for applause. The crowd's favorite was the second matador, tall and leggy, who could hug the bull's backside, he got so close.

Tristan looked over now and then at Joe. Joe did not react at all, mesmerized, or perhaps bored. Tristan got excited when the matador started doing little jumps and gestures, very dramatic. "Wow," he said, but nobody seemed to agree.

Mik said, "Those are just effects, *adornos*. They're considered vulgar, unless done right." Just then, the matador got on his knees before the bull. There was a little applause, but Tristan hesitated to clap, taking his cues from Mik and a lady in a row ahead of them who had bleached her hair blonde and had piled it high into the sky. Several people close to her seemed to depend on her, as well.

Watching the life drain from the beast was a decadent, splendorous evil. Most of the action occurred in the shade as the bull traveled across the ring, but every once in a while, a pitch-black bull would run out in the sunlight and the blood running down his back was an effect of chiaroscuro. Deep red, deep black, colors in a Nolde painting. That wasn't sweat he'd seen glistening, that was blood.

Revelations like that occurred all day in Nogales; it had a Spanish sense of severe baroque. Leather with brass studs, whips as decoration, a sense of aesthetic beauty out of pain, the blood on the black bull.

So, too, the painful pleasure of bullfighting. The sun beat down on his face; he'd paid for these kills. The bulls were snotting, frothing, then bleeding. Cigar smoke in his face, sun streaming.

How cruel it all was; the horses padded in a kind of mattress armor, but he could still see scars in their flanks where they'd been gored before. It was a horse's career.

Tristan thought: would I like such a moment, if I were a bull? The opportunity to die bravely? Was bravery not a necessity but something sought out? No, no. Tristan thought drag queens braver than matadors. Matadors were supposed to instill bravery in the bull, in the crowd.

Death came fast when the bull stumbled to its knees. A knife was plunged into its neck by one of the picadors. A team of horses, gaily festooned like a Rose Bowl float, trotted out to two men's whips, the bull was attached, paraded about and dispatched to God knows what rendering factory. Hoorah, and a kiss.

The rest of the kills did not run so smoothly. Two of the bulls were not brave and did not rise to the destiny they had coming, and a herd of tame bulls was released into the ring. The unbrave bull was absorbed into the herd and went out, presumably, to the humiliation of the pasture, a mild ignoble end, the real cruelty.

Sizzling in sun and tequila, Tristan had thought, I am not naturally virtuous. He knew virtue and it dazzled him, he loved it better than evil. There was a bull out there, he believed, that was naturally brave, that would come into the ring and not need the inciting of the matador; he would destroy the bullfights. He would be a revelation to these crowds.

And what about those without a fate or opportunity? The intermediaries of the world, born with neither choice nor destiny, like the blindfolded horses with snipped vocal cords? Brangäne in *Tristan und Isolde?* The servant. Mik. Who is the servant, and what of his destiny? But servants have power—to forgive, the ability to kill, or deliver fatal blows, like the horses. They are pivotal, neither subject nor object, an invisibility upon which everything depends.

But the bullfighters, if they were servants to the bulls, were inept that day in the ring. Tristan would never forget watching the last matador stab and stab at the wounded toro ineffectually, the blood and torture overwhelming, the crowd booing. People threw their Club de Leones cushions at the terrible matador, and the stabbing brought the tequila into Tristan's gorge, but it was Joe who puked all over the ugly rug.

They exited before the last trumpet drunkenly played.

After this tragic display of bad bullfighting, there seemed to be nothing more to do but leave. Tristan was the one who wanted to go, even though the sun was still high in the sky and they had earlier planned to paint the town red that night, maybe even staying over. Joe and Mik, like Tristan, had had enough of the phenomenally bad day in Nogales.

After passing through the inspection of a nosy lady at the border who wanted to know what all these drugs were for ("I have a cold," said Joe), they got in their car on the American side and headed due north, back to Tucson. They drove nearly half an hour before Mik started apologizing, as though the city of Nogales was all his fault. He was practically crying, he was so sorry. "It shouldn't have been that way; it should have been like a ballet. When they are good, you understand the necessity of *las corridas.* It should have been magic."

"Oh, no!" Joe interrupted him. It was an alarming sound.

"What?" Tristan asked.

Joe had slit open the box of AZT, the one consolation prize of the day, which cost two hundred dollars instead of five hundred. But inside, instead of the drug Joe needed, were bottles and bottles of a heart medication, perfectly legal in the States and useless to Joe. Later, they would find the antifungal and experimental irritant equally pointless.

Sometime during the bullfights, Mik had said something that made Tristan realize that the Punjabi friend was not gay, not an ex. Who was he, then? He liked to watch, apparently. Mik never drank or smoked or participated in the local religions. But he watched it all, Designated Driver, watched from the stands while the matador bloodied his own suit of light, while Joe faded into the sunset somewhere far north, as the Yaqui raised a crucifix, as his own parents returned to a homeland he'd never seen. Was he watching Tristan? Was he judging while he watched? And did his judgment have any real effect on anything in this world? What was that term in science, Tristan tried to remember, that Principle which stated that no study could be considered absolutely objective, because the observer always changed the observed? Heisman, Heimlich?

11

Dear Joe,

It's been four years since you took off for God knows where, and apparently I have lost more hair since you last saw me. Or so your sister tells me. Well, I'd like to see how well you would have aged, Saint Joe. I've seen pictures of your father. He had that stony-faced Mayan thing going on before he kicked. Die young, stay pretty, huh?

I'm here among your people again. Your mother and sister are being very nice to me, even though I feel like I'm causing a few problems. The biggest trouble happened earlier today at the Yaqui Easter Ceremonies, which you and I had always planned on watching but never quite got around to. There are these guys called Chapayekas, they're sort of the clowns, and they decided your sister was pretty. They did this little rape pantomime and your sister was not pleased.

It was kind of horrible; I don't blame her. There's another difference between men and women, though, because I would have loved to get gang-raped by a bunch of Chapayekas. Trouble is, now she won't be coming back to the ceremonies, and all I want to do is be there, watching.

I want to tell you about every move of this sometimes amazing, sometimes dull ritual, but it's hard to get a grip on it. I'm reminded of those huge narrative paintings of the Life of St. Ursula, in which you see a couple of people doing something on the left side of the painting, and by the time you walk to the other end of the picture, there they are again, doing something else, and you totally believe it's possible to see them twice in the same picture because so much time has passed since you saw them at the beginning.

You would have gotten a big kick out of the Matachinis, Joe. They are a bunch of guys who are sworn to serve the Virgin Mary, and so they dress like her. Nice outfits, skirts, and accessories out the wazoo.

Oh! And speaking of queens, you would not believe who's here! Father Dolan, the priest who performed your funeral! I know you never met him, but I feel like you two are close. Every time I'm near him, he's feeling guilty, like I caught him doing something he's not supposed to be doing, which is usually the case. For one thing, he's a closet queen. When I first talked to him at the wake for you, I talked to him like one homo to another, even if I never accused him of it directly. But he knew I knew. He kept talking about his serene whateverness, the Pope, the Vicar of Christ, to get away from the subject.

So here he is, working for the Yaqui village now. After the big Chapayeka assault on your sister, Mik took her home and I asked to be left behind, so I could check out the ceremony. Mik came back later to pick me up. While he was gone, I'm looking into the ramada of the church and there's Father Dolan, the Whitest Man in the World, with all these sweet brown people. What you should know about this thing is that it's one big sacrilege, as your mother would say. The Yaqui were converted to Catholicism way back, and because they were so remote, they went unsupervised a lot of the time, and dreamed up this big long ceremony reenacting the Passion of Christ. Everything's going along nice and religious-like, you get your Crucifixion, your Stations of the Cross, your Virgin Mary, and, then, all of a sudden, out pops the Deer Dancer!

Not exactly an official member of the Catholic pantheon. The Church itself seems to turn the other way, although the ceremonies require the participation of a priest, their priest. That would be Father Dolan. I sat there watching him with all these flag-bearing girls and a group of singers called the Maestros. His eyes kept darting around, like he was hoping his beloved Pope wasn't watching, or even the archbishop of the diocese.

I hadn't seen him in four years, but the second I poked my head in to wave at him, he immediately recognized me. From the look on his face, I might as well have been the Pope.

I don't know why I hate him so much, Joe. He's just a poor closet case who's very confused. But he's got one of those hit-me faces, you know; he makes me want to do violence to him. Kind of the way the Chapayekas wanted to work over your sister.

He's standing there and the Three Marys come up, little statues carried on litters, like queens. Everything is covered with flowers, real ones and fake ones. I had a thought about flowers I never thought of before, and that's this: after a long winter, there's nothing really to eat, and the only thing around, even in the desert, is flowers. We always think of flowers as a symbol of spring and rebirth, but they're also a symbol of hunger and poverty.

I watched him try to ignore all the playacting. The Fariseos and the Caballeros come in covered with black scarves—as if it isn't hot enough—and those crazy Chapayekas start sharpening their swords. Four guys in white robes take the statue of Jesus off the cross and carry it to Father Dolan, and the altar women and flag girls throw confetti all over it. Lots of confetti. Confetti, firecrackers, and flowers.

Lots of ritual, too, all this kneeling four times, and crossing themselves three times, and waving a flag ten times. They're always carrying some statue or other around town, at the Stations of the Cross.

There's a funny boy who keeps following me around. He's a friend of Mik, he's maybe thirteen, and already knows he's gay. Do you believe you can know such a thing at that age? I mean, fifteen, maybe. His name is Refugio and after Mik left to take Maria home, he became my guide, my little Virgil in the inferno.

He was interested in me because of you. Mik told him about you, and I think this kid is in love with you, or maybe this is that hero-worship thing.

I asked him, "So how do you know Mik?"

"He came to our village because he's with those historic preservation guys. He wants to know how he can help us save stuff. I know some of the deer songs and he likes to hear them."

It seems your little boyfriend is a good singer; he's got a *"tuik kutanak,"* a good throat.

Every once in a while, after four or five girls waved flags around and somebody chanted something, they'd lift up these little statues of the Three Marys on biers and just take off. Everybody in the village would get behind in a big parade with the Fariseos and the Chapayekas and what have you, and suddenly the stands would be totally cleared out and Refugio and I would be all alone, except for a couple of other people. I could tell he wanted to go with the rest of the village, but he wanted to talk to me even more. We sat on the bleachers and we could see them all in the distance going to each of the Stations of the Cross, all knocked down as part of the ritual, placed at the borders of the village. As soon as everybody was far away, he would ask me about you.

"How did you two meet?" he asked.

Do you remember, Joe, that bus shelter? I've always liked rainstorms because of that, how it forced us to stand close together, how we were immersed in water ever after.

I fell in love with you because you could make little figures out of a common handkerchief. In that bus shelter, you'd been entertaining yourself making a little hammock with two sausage-sized rolls of cloth nestled in the middle. My first words to you were, "Are those supposed to be babies?"

"Yes," you said. We spent those years together, lived together, wined and dined each other, and then you fell ill. Terminally. You lay in a bed. I revealed to you how superstitious I was. I prayed over your bed, within earshot: "If you let him live, I will attend church every day." But in a squeaky voice, you told me that, "This superstition is a kind of order; it's another kind of death." I didn't understand you. I thought you were delirious with fever.

On your deathbed, I said to you, "Please haunt me until I see you in the nether world. Every day, come into this room and make sure that I'm never with another person again in this world." You didn't agree to this, but you did pass away.

Weeks went by, and the haunting began. I'd be walking down Market Street when a paraplegic in a motorized wheelchair cut me off to ask for spare change. But since the paraplegic couldn't talk, he had an old toy ouija board in his lap and, with a pointer in his mouth, picked off the letters of his question. "S-P-A-R-E-

C-H-A-N-G-E." I shook my head, but I stayed to watch the poor guy spell out more. It was like watching a mystery being revealed. "J-O-K-E-S-W-E-L-C-O-M-E." Only, instead of pointing at the "K," he skipped it. "Joe's welcome." It was a visit from beyond.

Then there was our answering machine. I'd flipped the message tape over to make sure it wore evenly, and heard a message from you that I'd never heard before: "Hi. This is 563-0568. Neither Joe or Tristan is home right now, but if you want to leave us a message, we'll get back to you soon. Thanks, bye."

These words from beyond, these supernatural moments comforted me. Over the course of two years, I was visited by extra handkerchiefs in the laundry after going to the laundromat, raccoons on the roof at night, phones ringing once or twice and hanging up. It was you; it was cozy.

Then one night, I was sitting in an empty room reading a newspaper and your ghost came in. You were just a wisp of your former self, and you sat down on the floor, on top of my pile of already-read papers. "I'm here, like you asked," you said.

"Great," I said. I wasn't surprised. I'd been seeing the signs all along. But that night was bad planning on your part. "I was thinking of going out tonight, maybe to one of the bars, meeting somebody."

Your ghost looked pained. "Why do you want to do that? I thought you weren't interested in anybody during this short mortal life you're finishing up."

"Well, it seems longer now," I said. It did, too.

"Wait until you get a glimpse at eternity," you said, rolling your phantom eyes the way your sister does.

"I'm sorry I made you hang around. It's been two years; I think I can handle this on my own now." To be honest, I was a little disturbed.

"You can't go back on a promise," you said. "You begged me to stick around for the rest of your mortal existence." And Joe the ghost did. Wherever I went, your shade followed. To work, to restaurants, to the bathroom. I would pick up guys, and you would sit on the end of the bed and watch.

"This is really distracting," I would say in the heat of the moment, and my date would wonder what I was talking about. Then my date would go home, and I would be all alone again.

This went on, and I couldn't carry on anything serious, not with even the nicest guy.

Oh, Joe. This life is much longer than eternity, and, driven mad by the haunting, I killed myself to be away from you, because in this world I had hoped to love again, and it isn't possible. I've used up my romance quotient. I didn't know how much romance gets in the way of pleasure. I didn't correctly judge how much time can go by, and how it heals the ability to love, which is unbearable according to the parameters we set up.

That's what I told Refugio.

Refugio told me, "Oh, I don't believe in ghosts."

"Are you superstitious?" I asked him.

"What, you mean like *Psychic Friends Network?*" and I shrugged.

At your mother's house, Joe, she's tied up clear plastic produce bags full of water and hung them in windowsills and along the eaves. When I asked her what they were for, she said they were flytraps. The fly sees a magnified image of itself in the big balloon of water and gets scared away. This has to be a superstition. But then again, I haven't seen any flies, and the bags look sort of pretty, all shiny and wet. She dangles all sorts of things, hornet traps, bird feeders, wind chimes, little religious pendants, like Christmas ornaments on her big Christmas house.

I kept looking little pudgeball Refugio up and down and feeling kind of guilty for doing it. He was jailbait, right? I mean, I had no interest, but you know how people are; if somebody knows you're gay and they know one other gay person, all they can think of is the two of you getting together romantically. He was so thoroughly assured of his gayness I just assumed everybody in the village knew too, and I waited for them to pounce on me the second I so much as bumped into him. And then I also do that appraising thing; I'm always trying people on for size. Even your brother-in-law, even your sister, I look them over and I think, how would it be to share a life with this person? To sleep and eat with them, to touch them. It's my omnivorous habit. I'm always trying to see every passing situation as permanent. Remember how you made me stay at home while you picked out our apartment? Every dump was going to be just fine by me.

After we watched several more ritualistic clownings by the Pascolas, one of them came up to Refugio and me and offered us cigarettes. They were all passing out cigarettes, to people in the crowd, to people in the ceremony. Everybody was lighting up. Refugio later told me that this was part of the ritual.

Refugio didn't know who was behind the mask, but the Pascola knew him. "Hey, Refugio, you old Caballero, what are you doing smoking? Minors can't smoke."

"I'm no Caballero, I'm a Matachini," Refugio protested. The Pascola dancer had an oval mask of wood painted black with little white flower designs all around and a beard. He flicked a lighter and Refugio took a drag. He lit for me but he wouldn't talk to me.

"Listen, Caballero, who is your white friend here with the big butt? May I give your friend a comb for his beautiful abundant hair?"

"I'm no Caballero," Refugio said again, and blew smoke into the mask of the Pascola.

The Pascola gave me a comb. "For your beautiful abundant hair." Just before he walked away from us, he said to me, "White man, your little friend here has a beautiful throat. Tell him I apologize for calling him Caballero."

Refugio has sworn a vow to be a Matachini. He's bound his head with a bright blue bandanna, then he's got red crepe paper all over this bamboo hat. There are all these streamers draping off that, and paper flowers. He drags around this gourd rattle in one hand and what looks like a feather duster in the other. He's a lucky one who gets to wear a dress, too, long, white, but you can see his pants under the skirt and a bright red sash. He also likes to fidget with about fifty strings of cheap Mardi Gras beads hung around his neck. When he and the rest of the Matachinis dance, it looks like they're doing the Virginia Reel, especially since they dance to fiddles and guitars.

"I should be a Deer Singer, but I made a *manda,*" he told me.

"A *manda?*" I asked.

"When you are sick and you think you're going to die, you say, I'll be a Matachini if only you will let me live. When I got better, I said, it is proper now for me to make a promise."

"So what did you have that made you so sick?"

Refugio kicked a little dirt and said, "Worms or something." Then he looked up and said, "Hey, look. *Maso.*"

He was pointing at the Deer Dancer.

To me, the Deer Dancer is the embodiment of being old. He's got that stuffed deer on his head and he wears this shawl around his waist over rolled-up jeans. He's got those gourd rattles, and if he put them up to his chest, they'd look like breasts.

He was dancing. Putting a lot of energy into it. His hands are nearly to the ground and he sticks his butt out and arches his back like he's imitating a street sign that says, "Dangerous Curve."

Refugio says that the songs the three singers were performing didn't talk about Jesus or God at all. "They're about flowers and the place where the deer lives." Suddenly, this little pork sausage kid opens up his mouth and he starts singing along. It's unearthly. Repeats itself over and over again and you want it to go forward, but after a while, you don't want it to end. It's all Yaqui, not Spanish. People started looking at Refugio, because he had a nice voice. That made Refugio stop, because he didn't want to ruin the dancing.

"What did you just sing?" I asked Refugio.

"You who do not have enchanted legs, what are you looking for, what are you looking for?"

The song was changing.

"Now what does the song say?"

"Over there, in the middle of the flower-covered wilderness, you who do not have enchanted legs, what are you looking for?"

I almost tried to answer the question myself. Suddenly, the Pascola who'd given a cigarette to a minor and called him a Caballero started trying to trip up the Deer Dancer. I felt like going up and kicking his butt. Everybody was laughing at the Deer Dancer, but he never got upset, he just kept shaking his rattle and sniffing around with his deer head.

"Enchanted legs? Why are they saying that?" I was feeling so stupid, but I needed to know.

Refugio enjoyed watching. "Maybe the song is about how the deer has lost his magic. Maybe he is a little clumsy. Maybe he is looking for his magic; he is looking for his ability to dance again."

I was really enjoying that cigarette. I felt completely guilty when Mik caught me with it. I stubbed it out. "Look how old he is." I pointed at the Deer Dancer for Mik. "How is Maria?"

"She's fine. It just surprised her. I stayed a long time with her because she wanted some tea and she just wanted to talk about it. I think she understands now."

Refugio handed up to Mik the last of his cigarette. Mik was very gracious and took a drag and handed it back to Refugio. When in Rome, I guess. He said to Refugio, "I'm going to have to take your new friend home because we're tired. We'll see you tomorrow?"

I wasn't tired. I wanted to stay all night.

Refugio said sure.

When we walked out of the plaza, I could see the stars again. What a time for the skies, Joe, you wouldn't believe it. This comet, it's a sign from the future. And out here, away from all the big city lights, I'll look up and there'll be these steady, tiny, swift lights that look like stars but they're heading somewhere important. They have to be satellites—that's all they could be. Dozens of them.

Now I've come home and it's very late, nearly two in the morning. I'm in your mother's bed-and-breakfast and Murphy is staying with me. The Murphster, always glad to see me. Right now he's on his back on the bed and the fan is blowing on his belly and his privates, which cools him off. I just noticed that Murphy isn't fixed. All that money your mom has spent on this poor dog, and she never cut his balls off. What do you suppose that is about? Does she think it's every animal's duty to procreate?

She has no idea I'm positive. It's harder to keep it away from her now, now that I may be living a lot longer. That's a good thing, but it's not all fun and games, you know, Joe. I mean, I've been planning not to plan for the future. Life sure as hell was easier to live when it looked like there wasn't any life left. Now I have to be circumspect. Careful. That's just not my style, Joe.

You are probably pissed that I don't tell anybody. But what good would it do? I'd have to hold your mother's hand while she fretted about me, and she wouldn't see how happy I was, and there's really nothing interesting about it. All those San Francisco activist boys would lynch me, saying it's my duty to be visible. But they just don't seem to see how the only really juicy part of the story is the scary part that they won't discuss themselves: how the hell they got it. Not, you know, some guy stuck it in me and didn't have a rubber on. Anybody can tell that story, and they'll probably lie about that, too. But what the hell was in our heads, when we knew full well, when everybody knows full well.

It's hubris, isn't it, Joe? Sheer assholish pride, the same pride that keeps you from cutting a dog's balls off or inspires you to start your own ceremony about Jesus' Crucifixion that's several days long and breaks all the rules. It's the one thing that makes things happen.

And who can tell that story of my own hubris, or yours? It's an awesomely dark story about a prolonged mistake. And even if you told it just slightly wrong, it merely sounds like a case of suicide.

Got to go sleep. More later! I miss you. Love, Tristan.

*   *   *

Tristan wrote all of this in his little notebook. Why, he wondered, was he so excited about somebody else's beliefs? Yes, it was like opera, and for a moment, he thought of Kundry, the harlot in *Parsifal* who had laughed at Christ on the cross and was doomed to live forever: how Wagner gave the evil Klingsor the power to resurrect her, and how she shrieked upon reawakening into this world.

Did Christ come back from the dead and shriek as well? There was not a little horror to being dragged away from eternal peace.

He paced the room. Mrs. Jimenez had hung a crucifix in each room. But how much did she believe? He'd found in the magazine stand a coffee table book called *Decorating in a Spiritual Style.*

There wasn't much of God left that wasn't an antique shop find or a bit of camp kitsch.

And why was Joe all wrapped up in this? Why could he only describe the Yaqui Easter to a dead man? Was he appealing to Joe as an intercessor? Joe as saint again: if he were on a prayer card, he'd appear as a wizard with a tall cone-shaped hat and a fizzing wand, or maybe in a tuxedo, pulling a rabbit out of a top hat.

He made a whole pot of tea, but fell asleep while it was steeping, and never drank it.

12

Maria picked Tristan up on Saturday morning and brought him back to her house so he could catch up with the kids and Earl.

Joe and Tristan had had at least one good laugh at Maria's hubby's name. But he wasn't terrible. He seemed to love Maria with all his heart, or might, without making protestations. He liked the kids, and didn't try to hide the fact from himself that he knew he had a big homo in his house for lunch and Easter egg coloring on Saturday.

"Maria always says you two have a lot in common," Earl said while he made mixed drinks for himself and Tristan. It was after noon, he'd said, time to drink. He made whiskey sours. Mixed drinks, Tristan thought; I haven't had mixed drinks in years. Martinis, neat scotch, sure, but fluffy things from a blender seemed campy. Would Earl want to talk about golf next? "So I'm hoping you and me can talk man to man, so I can figure out how that girl's brain works."

The oldest of their two sons came in. "Dad, *Pocahontas* is over. We want to watch again."

"You know how to rewind, Boss."

"No, we want you to do it."

Maria said to Tristan, "Earl's out on the road for three days at a time. When he's home, they want to hog him up."

Earl handed Tristan the whisky sour. Tristan tasted it. He thought about the saldito, which he'd wrapped in a gum wrapper deep in his pocket, for a future attempt. Earl excused himself to the den, where the VCR was.

Tristan wondered whether this was a good time to discuss the Chapayeka situation. "Are you all right?" he asked Maria.

She waved off the problem, and her hand was a demonstration of a diver's clean jackknife into a pool. "Oh yeah," she said, "Old news."

Tristan didn't want to press her. She was so refreshing, unwilling to process all day like the women he knew in San Francisco. She'd go on. Sure, she'd boycott the Yaqui ceremonies but he'd bet she'd never employ a therapist. The mock rape would be her private terror, and she'd value it as such. Maria would forever dot her exclamation points with stars.

She said, "Come on, let me show you the dogs."

Oh yes, the dogs. He'd forgotten that Earl's hobby was raising show dogs. For a while it was dachshunds, then beagles. "Lately," Maria said, "he's turned to springer spaniels. He's got this one, named Maria, that's been picking up every prize. She's a real winner."

"I'd love to see a prizewinner."

"Oh, Maria isn't here; she's never here. She's with Don and Lisa, the managers, on the road."

"Earl doesn't show them himself?"

"Oh, no. He hardly ever sees his dogs when they're showing."

They walked out of the fiercely air-conditioned house into the desert heat and Tristan watched his drink glass begin to sweat. Maria led him to the barn and a big patch of grass (Earl's *yard*, Maria called the desert miracle) and then around to a second pole barn. He could hear the baying as they approached.

He was shocked at first. Out in a chicken wire pen were eight beagles climbing over each other to get near Maria and Tristan. They were panting and howling. One had some terrible skin problem and its fur was coming off in patches. Tristan looked up at the sun, just to see if he was hallucinating. There wasn't a single place in the pen to get out of the direct light.

"These are the beagles," Maria said. "That one with the red choke was a big national champ three years ago."

"What's his name?"

Maria made a yikes! contortion of the corners of her mouth. "Gosh, what? Moxie? Molly? Check on the plaque over the hutch when we go inside—it's there." Tristan hunkered down and put his hand through the mesh and let the eight nameless dogs lick the sweat and salt off it.

"Come on," Maria motioned. There was more to see. There were three stalls in the pole barn, each one a pen for at least as many dogs as the clambering beagles out in the sun. The dachshunds growled like old ladies; they had bourbon barks. They didn't crawl all over each other. They just paced to the four corners of the stall like fish in a bowl. But Tristan noticed that the barn was kept remarkably clean. He said so.

"That's the boys' jobs," Maria said. "Earl gives them a dollar for every full bag of doggy doodoo. The boys call them doodoo dollars." She laughed.

Tristan thought the dogs that lived in the pole barn might be better off than the ones in the pen because at least they could avoid the sun. But now he recalled a science lesson about why Venus was hotter than Mercury, even though Mercury was closer to the sun. The roof of the barn was like a cloudy atmosphere that held heat in. It was suffocating.

The last stall was like the Island of Dr. Moreau, the failed breeding experiments of a mad scientist. There was a limping cocker spaniel, an old Jack Russell, two poodles that half-heartedly tried to mount each other. In the back of the stall was a barrel sawed in half and full of water for the dogs. It was jellied over and deep with algae. This was the part, thought Tristan, where the rookie cop sees the body and tosses his cookies. Tristan took a swallow of his mixed drink.

Maria seemed unfazed by the conditions. He was afraid to ask her questions like who walked the dogs, did they get groomed, did the water get changed. He was a guest, and might not like the answers. Easier topics: sex, politics, and religion.

Maria took him back to the house bragging about how successful the dog show had been for Earl. He was almost able to give up trucking.

"He'd be home more often. Can you stand that?" Tristan asked with a sly look.

"Oh sure," she said, not wanting to joke about it. "He's great with the boys and he's my soul mate. The bed is so empty when he's on the road." But as she said it, Tristan could see she was thinking of *his* empty bed, feeling sorry for him.

Mondays had been Tristan's night out when Joe was alive—or rather, Tristan's night in, alone. Joe would go bowling with the very *pesado* Charles, and Tristan would blast *The Pixies* or *Die Walküre* on the stereo and order pizza delivery and read poetry out loud and drink almost a whole bottle of wine himself. He'd loved it.

Four years now and every day had been boy's night alone, and it was like playing tennis without boundary lines. It must be what's wrong with being rich, he suddenly thought.

Earl came out on the deck to greet them. "Aren't they beauties?" he said, "Oh, but you're a cat person."

"No, no!" said Tristan. Not at all. "In fact, I've been looking for a Jack Russell. How about selling me that one?" He waved at the barn, and meant it. He had visions of himself and his pet, meeting people in the park. And he had another more vicious little image of himself saying tenderly and eerily to the animal, stroking it as he did so, "I'm going to outlive you, too."

"Oh, I couldn't," Earl said. "I got him because I thought the Kennel Club was going to approve them as an official breed. It was a gamble. No dice. But I'm so attached, you know. I couldn't part with any of them."

"You mean you don't have a pet?" asked Maria. "Oh, you should have a pet. You could call it Monkey," she smiled. Somewhere along the way, Tristan thought, Maria's hard work at creating this private joke about the pet monkey had lost its ability to bind them together.

"Your mom seems pretty happy with the Murphster," said Tristan. Only Tristan called Murphy the Murphster, he realized.

Maria rolled her eyes. "If she spent half the money on AIDS research as she does on that mutty rat, there'd be a cure already."

Earl tightened his lips in agreement, or maybe it was a pleased expression—some facial expression he'd thought of and she'd adopted.

"How is she?" Tristan asked. "Really."

Husband and wife gave each other the United Front glance.

"Inconsistent," Earl said. "Goes whole hog, and then drops it. Drops a thousand bucks on an orphan and then ignores it."

"It's a family trait," Maria said. She was reaching into the cupboard and pulled out a big blue bowl. "Look, Tristan! The bowl!"

It was that wedding gift. Truth to tell, Joe and Tristan had picked it out of a mail order catalog and had it shipped by phone. "Oh, yeah," said Tristan.

Earl put a meaty hand on Tristan's shoulder. Tristan kept thinking, that gesture must take him some doing. "Boss, it meant a helluva lot to us, that bowl. It was the only thing we got."

"You're kidding."

Maria sighed. "It's still a sore point around here," she explained. "Nobody thought we'd last. They still don't. I've been married to Earl longer than I was with Tom, and my mother still thinks I'm shacking up."

Tristan was shocked. But he loved being shocked, because so little could shock him in perpetually naughty San Francisco. The problem with naughtiness was that it killed the power of gossip. He even had to leave the city to get good graffiti. On a bathroom stall in the Phoenix airport he'd read, "Will suck your dick, call 268-4390, beeper number 850-2411." Somebody had written below, "Jeez, do you have a Web site?" and the initial desperado had returned to mirthlessly add, "No, I don't, so just call." Now it had slipped Tristan's mind, how he could shock Joe's family by saying what he thought were ordinary observations, how there was no jealousy left in his life, that if men dated him but dated others as well, he didn't mind. This was so foreign to Maria, who wanted so much to have everything in common with him, that she'd been struck dumb. And now it was payback time, the shock of grudges, slow acceptance, heartless but sheltering morality.

She turned to Earl, sat in his lap. "But it was all for true love, wasn't it, honey?" She put her arm around her tall husband's thick waist. "You know how that is, right, Tristan? That's what we both know for sure—you can't not fall in love."

They all knew how Tristan had been HIV negative and fell for Joe, even knowing Joe was positive. Maria thought this was a romantic wonder, like marrying a foreigner, or a Hindu.

"It's relentless," said Maria. "You just become so selfish. I felt blindfolded when I fell for Earl, couldn't see a thing, had to feel it all."

"How romantic," Earl said. Tristan thought, that's where she's learned to roll her eyes like that.

She used the embracing arm to smack him in the gut. "It is! At least Tristan understands."

"Drugs," Earl said. "Her mother thought she was on drugs."

Whenever people did inscrutable things, they were always explained as drug-induced.

"I don't believe she's still mad," said Tristan.

Maria nodded, oh, yes, she is. "Just little things now and then, just to let me know."

She gave Maria's firstborn son more expensive birthday presents. But when that oldest boy also lost his first baby tooth, he happened to be staying overnight at his grandmother's. When the Tooth Fairy came there, it left a five-dollar bill—expensive precedent.

"She wants to ruin us on baby teeth!" Earl said.

Tristan shrugged. "Maybe she just loves those kids. She likes paying attention to people. She didn't book anybody in the B and B all the time I'm there, because she wanted to spend time with me. I must be costing her two hundred bucks a night."

Maria did a get-outta-here wave. "Is that what you think? She's just a space shot. People call to make reservations and she just doesn't bother calling them back."

This was news to Earl, too. "Sheesh. I wish I could afford to hemorrhage money like that."

Maria said, "Well, she can afford to be the Tooth Fairy at five bucks a pop. It's from that big insurance return she got from Joe's policy."

"Joe's policy?"

Maria nodded. "Surprised Mom, too. All that time, he'd been paying on a policy. She got a couple hundred thousand."

At the time that this bomb was dropped, Tristan only nodded at the consolation prize. It only tickled his mind with injustice, and he thought, but what about me? It was over the next days, and weeks, that the rage grew. But for now, he just grumbled. We were partners. Joe never told Tristan a thing about a policy. Why didn't Joe leave him something? Why hadn't anybody told him about this? How magnanimous Mrs. Jimenez had looked when she wrote a check for the funeral expenses.

Maria said, "She said she'd give it all up just to talk with him for five minutes."

There was macaroni and cheese, salad, and green beans from Mrs. Jimenez's garden. Maria boiled water and took two cartons of eggs out of the refrigerator. She'd written in magic marker, "HARD BOILED" on the cartons. She placed them one by one into the big blue bowl. "We use it all the time," she said. She prepared all the egg decorating materials and then she called her sons up to do the coloring.

Two dark-haired kids, eight and six years old, shot up the stairs. Other than the hair, they hardly resembled each other. The youngest one had a pacifier in his mouth and was asked to remove it at the table. "Do you know where we get the Easter Bunny?" the older one said by way of introducing himself to Tristan. "It's a pagan tradition."

Earl said, "He's smart. Obviously not my kid."

Mostly, Maria's sons were well-behaved. Tristan quizzed them. He felt self-conscious around children, wondering whether even Maria allowed the broader meaning of the word "pervert" to enter her mind. He was always careful not to touch children, not out of fear of infecting them, not even from a real attraction, but because he never wanted to be misunderstood.

They liked Tristan's attention, though. He was called Uncle Tristan by Maria but it didn't really stick. Tristan kept looking at their mouths, round, red, open fish-mouth frowns of concentration and maybe a little swollen unhealthiness, virulent, like they might give him something. Little rubber rings of fat that seemed vaguely pornographic to him. Children were such potential victims. To a child, everybody was a magician.

Halfway through the egg coloring, a very old man fell into the room. Earl said, "Good morning, Dad. How ya doing?" and got his aged parent a seat.

Earl's father was what they meant when they said "palsied." He
trembled from every possible joint, and when his son made him a
7 and 7, Tristan watched intently to see if he could bring the drink
to his lips without spilling it. So far, though, it was clumsy Tristan
who'd done all the spilling, typically trying to do too many things
at once. He had a cheese spot on his T-shirt and later, when he tried
to color an egg while knocking back his drink, it fell hard into the
cup of coloring and cracked. The purple dye italicized the crack
and even the kids laughed at his klutzy mistake.

"I'm Tristan," he introduced himself to Earl's father.

The old man muttered something Tristan couldn't hear and
knew would never hear no matter how many times he repeated it.

The youngest son said, "There's an eyelash or something in my
macaroni."

Helpless youth on his left, helpless dotage on his right, who is
going to take care of us all? Tristan wondered. He'd had that
panicky feeling often: who would be left to take care of him when
he got sick? Was it his main motivation for remaining sociable,
making new friends?

Earlier, in the truck ride to Maria's house, she made some
observations that made him realize they assumed he led a solitary
life. All his friends croaking, away from his own family, he must
be holing up in some kind of monastic cell.

"What do you do to keep from always thinking about it?" was
what she asked.

"Surround myself," he'd said. "I teach all day, meet somebody
for dinner after that. At home I gab on the phone and the stereo is
always on." This empty silent desert was the real challenge.

"Don't take it wrong," said Maria after he'd said that and she
thought about it, "but I pray to God I never get to the end of
romance. I don't have all those things to drown out the noise. I'd
go nuts."

"You've got kids," Tristan said. "You've got religion. You've
got Mom. Mik."

Now, at the dinner table, he thought of adding that the end of
romance isn't bleak or depressing, it's just unmagical. It requires a
little imagination or memory, or some combination. Avoiding

despair, that's the thing. Trying to fight down the destructive notion that time was nothing but an enemy.

"We got Web TV," said the boy with hair in his macaroni. Mom had omnipotently saved that situation by taking the plate to the sink, removing the hair, moving the food around a little out of the kid's eyeshot, and returning it to the table. *"Cuidado,"* she said. "It's hot."

"What's Web TV?" Tristan asked.

The kid snorted with disdain; Tristan recognized it as a learned grade-school response. "You don't know?"

Dear Joe, he thought to himself. He was always writing these imaginary letters to Joe, as if he were simply on vacation, or in the Peace Corps, or scaling Everest. Dear Joe, there's this new thing called Web TV. Dear Joe, O.J. Simpson was accused and tried for murder. Dear Joe, everywhere you look, it says www.something. com. Oh, how much Tristan resented fashion! He considered pop music an atrocity. How dare the world be filled with the pabulum of blockbuster movies, catchy advertising slogans, and bestselling novels, and not let Joe know about them?

The kids, like kids, were suddenly bored with egg coloring. They took Tristan to the den while Maria cleaned up. They showed him Web TV. They could type faster than he could.

"When I was a boy," Tristan said, "typing was considered a girl thing. If you were a good typist, you were called a sissy." Tristan had been.

"We don't call it typing. We call it keyboarding."

Tristan was not alarmed by all this www.something.com. It looked like typing was coming back into style.

Earl came down with a fresh drink. "She's nuts about you," he confided again.

"She's nuts about you," Tristan said back.

"I'm nuts about her." Earl took a drink. "But she scares me, you know. Hot and cold. She says she's nuts about you becáuse you two are exactly alike. Exactly. So if you don't mind my asking, Mister Identical Twin, how do I make sure what she did to her first she doesn't do to me?"

Tristan's response was meant to comfort him, but might not have been the answer the guy wanted to hear. "She's not going to go. She's had enough." In his mind, he was thinking of the poor dogs. The dogs wouldn't leave either. Despite the algae-lined water trough. "Joe has suspended her in time. She's Sleeping Beauty. She's got something to prove to you."

Earl thanked him, but his face was all screwed up. He'd wanted more, some secret password. Was the loss of Joe something that was supposed to have made Tristan a wise sage? On the contrary, Tristan felt stupid. Dumbed down.

"It must be tough being alone," said Earl. He was terrified of Tristan, Tristan realized. He was Earl's worst nightmare.

"I'm not alone. Don't tell Maria, but I've been with somebody for about a year." Tristan thought maybe Earl would like that secret, at least—even if it was a lie. One that he made up right there, without thinking. Or perhaps it was the beginning of his revenge—for not getting the insurance money. It was later that night that he realized that this imaginary boyfriend was a vengeful construct, forged from a quiet devastation and confusion: Saint Joe? Would a saint be secretive with the insurance money?

But Earl didn't like the secret. "Oh, really? It must seem kind of broken down, huh? Can't hold a candle to old Joe. Must be hard not to compare."

Tristan was vexed, and let himself say, "Maria and I have a lot in common."

"Whoosh," said Earl. It was the sound of being buzzed by a jet plane. "Okay, I get it. Whoosh."

Tristan held his glass of booze out as a toast, or an apology—it's the liquor talking. "No, Earl, that's the thing. I never do compare — it's a different animal. Not better or worse, *más o menos fuerza*. He's so totally different from Joe, maybe there's something weird in that." Please, Tristan was begging in his head, just ask me his name. Just care a little.

But Earl relaxed against the couch back, exhausted. "So do you think the city will vote in a new 'Niners stadium?"

Tristan shrugged, watched images flash on the Web TV. "You Don't Know Jack," it said.

"I think the thing to watch out for with Maria," he said, "is too much enthusiasm. If she keeps saying I love it, I love it, or you, you, that means she's trying to convince herself of something she doesn't really believe."

Maria came down the stairs just as he finished saying that and he prayed she hadn't overheard. "This chair is incredibly comfortable," he said, just to say something to make it seem like they'd not talked about anything.

"It's my favorite, too," said Maria, pushing Earl at the shoulder. "See, silly," she said. "You didn't want to buy it, but people with good taste love it, see?"

13

All through the breakfast at Maria's, the subject of the Chapayeka rape scene—for that was what Tristan called it in his head—did not come up again after his initial query. It was too weird and awful to be acknowledged, but what was very clear was that Maria had had enough, and would not be returning. This proved to be a dilemma for Tristan. He had been drawn into the Yaqui ceremony, and wanted to see as much as he could. But Maria had set aside her whole weekend for him.

When it finally came time for Tristan to choose, he said, "Maria, I don't expect you to go with me. But I'd like to see a little more."

"Tristan!" she said, and in her voice was the message: "Don't be silly, of course you should go. But will you promise to come over afterwards and visit with me?"

"You can't have dinner with me on Easter?"

She shook her head. "Sorry, family commitments." She stuck a thumb in Earl's direction; Earl was glued to a ball game of some sort on the tube. "If you come, we'll make Earl cook."

"Earl can cook?" Tristan said it loud in order to bait him.

"Watch out, Boss," Earl said from his slump, never letting his eyes leave the set. Ooh—was it a threat or a promise?

Mik, who had spent the morning downtown at his office, had come by to take Tristan back to the Easter Ceremony. He stepped in the door and the two boys rammed up to him and each grabbed a pantleg. "Mr. Wizard!" they yelled.

"Hello, boys," Mik said, speaking to them more as if they were adults, or colleagues. "I have come to take Uncle Tristan away from you. Or will you fight me for him?"

The boys (the youngest had a pacifier in his mouth again) let go of the pantlegs and the oldest said, "We're lovers, not fighters."

"Good men," said Mik.

"Do the boys want to go with us?" Tristan asked.

Maria said, "They get bored. And they're a handful. You don't want to keep track of them when you're trying to enjoy it."

"Lovers, not fighters, lovers, not fighters, lovers, not fighters," the little one said, trying out the phrase for himself.

Tristan got into Mik's car. Today, the front seat was piled with books and files with important initials all over them: SHPO, ISTEA, WRO. Secret languages, any, made Tristan want to know. "I was remembering the bullfights in Nogales," he said to Mik. "Do you remember that day, when they shaved my eyebrows?"

"And Joe got the wrong drugs? I've beaten myself up every day for not driving back to exchange them. It could have made a big difference."

"Mik, if I beat myself up for every shortcoming I had with Joe, I'd be dead by now. On the day before Joe died, I made him peel potatoes in bed. He said he was feeling useless, and that was my stupid solution. I'm sure it wore him out. Killed him."

"Yes, but this involved medicine."

"No, it involved money. He could get all the drugs he needed in San Francisco; they just weren't cheap."

"Too bad these new drugs weren't around."

"Yes."

"Have you ever seen them?"

Tristan nodded. "I have a friend who was way gone to dementia. We had him on twenty-four-hour surveillance because he went out one day and bought a Mercedes and a BMW on the same day. Then he started taking the protease inhibitors and jeez, Mik, he's come back. He's working again, going to the gym, all of it. And it's weird. He says he remembers every minute, perfectly."

"The afterlife."

"We don't know what to do. We're all so used to saying bye-bye with such finality, we don't know how to carry on any more. It was easier having friendships with some of these guys because it seemed so short term. You can forgive a person's foibles easier if they're on their last legs."

Mik drove along silently. Was he bored? Angry? Memorious? "Have you been down to Nogales for any more bullfights?" Tristan asked.

Mik sighed. "I gave them up."

"Gave them up? What? Like smoking?"

"Joe was right. They're cruel and wrong."

"Oh, Joe just says things. Said. Joe used to kick dogs if they got in our garden."

"Nevertheless. I have other hobbies."

Like what, Tristan wondered. All along the road heading into Pascua, there was an increase in bathtub grottoes and roadside shrines. "Look at them all," Tristan remarked. Most had the Virgin Mary ensconced within a robin's-egg-blue half-sphere of upended tub, sunk into the baked earth. Garlands of flowers, some plastic, some real, were draped over them, and often there were strings of Christmas lights, candles, little natural fetishes.

"There was one in my yard when I bought my house," said Mik. "It was a sight. *San Ygnacio, un santo muy po-pu-lar aquí.* Well done. Wooden statue, little icons, candles. Red lights that I could switch on and off at the front door. I decided to keep it, since somebody had worked so hard on it, and I wanted to blend in with the neighbors. I'd turn the lights on at night and it made a good light to keep bugs from going into my house and it helped people walk up my front steps without tripping.

"But I had this problem. Lowlifes kept coming to the door. They'd ring the doorbell at about one in the morning and I'd come out in my bathrobe and these scruffy-looking guys would get bug-eyed and just back right away, turn, and run. This went on for a few weeks, not all the time, but often enough to make me worried. I thought, what kind of barrio have I moved into? They never looked like they were going to rob me or beat me up, but they were always a little bit *borracho,* or messed up, and they always ran off when they saw me."

Tristan could imagine one of these guys standing in the lurid red light of the bathtub grotto, the look of terror at the sight of Mik—

that big long hair could look pretty wild if he'd slept on it a little. "Was it always men?" He suspected something sexual, that other guys had suspected Mik of being gay just as he had.

"No. Sometimes a guy and a girl, all huggy, looking like they expected to find a party at my house. They'd be friendlier when they backed down off the stoop, and they'd say, 'Oops, sorry, wrong house.' "

"It was the grotto, wasn't it?" Tristan said.

Mik nodded. "Some neighbor finally came over, must've seen me getting called on one night and he explained it to me. A known drug dealer in the barrio used to live there, and his signal to let his customers know he was open for business was when he turned on the red lights on the grotto."

Tristan had to laugh. "What would the Virgin Mary think?"

"She'd be pissed," Mik said, but obviously he'd already had his big laugh over this a long time ago. "Naturally, I had to dismantle the thing. My parents didn't like it very much anyway, even when I tried to explain its cultural and historical significance."

They'd parked by now; Mik had roved the lot looking in vain for a shady place so the car wouldn't become a furnace while they were away from it. When they resigned themselves to a death by fire, they were able to grab a space very close to the end of the Plaza. There was that massive effigy of Judas hung across a frame of wood. He was stuffed with so many firecrackers that it made Tristan wince just thinking about them going off. Firewood was stacked up high like a teepee all around Judas.

"*Fuego,*" he marveled.

Still and ever deadpan, Mik said, "The Sonoran desert was once a vast forest."

The village was remarkably more crowded today. There was more activity in the plaza and in the ramada of the church as well. Everybody was dressed in Sunday best, which heightened for Tristan the poignant sense of dignity amidst the shabbiness, houses often constructed of discarded railroad ties, corrugated sheet metal, daub, even flattened-out tin cans.

Mik strode along. He wasn't really looking around at the circus, and Tristan allowed himself to think that Mik was never interested in the journey, just the arrival, just the just-to-say-we-did-it. He's got an ugly gait, Tristan thought. He looks like an ape, or that spooky film of Bigfoot the guy took on horseback.

Mik stopped, as if he could hear Tristan's bad thoughts. "So Maria says you told Earl you've got a new boyfriend."

When Tristan got ready to say the word "Well," he kept his lips in the shape for saying "oooo," and hesitated before saying the word, his eyebrows two perfect humps. "Well, I didn't think he was listening."

"Why didn't you tell us about him? Why didn't you bring him along?"

Tristan shook his head, "No, no, Mik, there's nobody. I told Earl that to make him . . . to see what he would say."

"What did he say?"

"Nothing, just like I thought he would. Plus, if I remember correctly, I asked him to keep it a secret."

"There's really nobody?"

"Really. I'm past my prime now. And you know, I had the great love. All the rest would be shoe salesmen."

"Apparently you made quite an impression on Refugio. Look, here he comes."

Refugio had been standing around some unlaid drainpipes with a few other Matachini. When he spotted Mik and Tristan, he jumped off his own pipe and lifted his white skirt and meandered toward them. He looked like he was in no hurry, but he was obviously happy to see his two gringo friends.

"I've got something for you gringos," said Refugio. He had, tucked into his red sash, two ice-cream-cone-sized items with decorated eggs where the scoops ought to be. "Cascarones."

"These are great," said Mik. "Did you make them yourself?"

Refugio nodded. They were trimmed with ribbons and anointed with glue and glitter. On Tristan's, he'd painted the head of Bart Simpson. For Mik, he'd painted a bullfighter in his *traje de luces.* "Inside the egg, there's confetti. You break it open during the big battle and shake it all over the place."

"It looks too pretty to break," said Tristan.

Refugio was agitated by this. "No, you have to. It's the tradition."

It was hot as hell; there was no better cliché for it. And those Caballeros and Chapayekas and Maestros and Fariseos were wearing all those clothes and blankets and masks. Many of the spectators had umbrellas, and if they didn't, they jury-rigged some shade. One old lady had an unused disposable diaper on her head. Jury-rigged was the word for everything.

The ceremony itself, Tristan sometimes thought, was being made up as they went along.

"Today is the big day," said Refugio. "Everything happens. All the bad people are beaten and they are brought back to Jesus. I have to go and get ready." He ran off and promised to see them after things calmed down. He made Tristan promise he'd come and watch the maypole ceremony.

Tristan shook his head at Mik. "I don't understand it. He's completely comfortable being who he is with his people. And they don't seem to mind one bit." He didn't understand, and, in a way, he resented it. He couldn't quite get his mind wrapped around the idea of these people just accepting a pubescent boy's oddness. He'd never say so aloud, but Refugio reminded Tristan a lot of himself at that age, his build, his slight nerdiness, his ease with adults.

"You mean his being gay? Well, he doesn't go around trumpeting it. And this is his family. He has duties, public and civic duties, only he can understand why, in such a small community. They may be poor, but they have plenty of community. I'm jealous. I'm jealous of you gays up there in San Francisco for having all that community. Don't your people have big celebrations you feel part of?"

My people, Tristan wondered? Did he feel like waving giddily with relief every time he saw a car's bumper with a rainbow flag sticker on it? "My people," he said. "I don't really fit in with my people." You'd think we'd be more complex, as a people. But instead of being a guy or a girl, which is about as complicated as it gets in the regular world, we have one more adjective. Instead of being one dimensional, gays can *almost* handle two. Screaming queen, leather daddy, dumb blonde, AIDS widow, trans vestite. Put one more adjective in there, and homos go into a tailspin. Catholic leather daddy just ruins the fantasy.

"Let me ask you something, Mik. What did you think when Maria ran off on Tom in the ninth month of her pregnancy, and then married Earl?"

It was Mik's turn to say, "Well." Then he said, "I certainly didn't buy them a big blue bowl."

Mik, Tristan realized somewhere, had endured, like Tristan, a lifetime of rudenesses. He had survived by believing in efficiencies, like a human body nourishing itself and then voiding. Gifts, he'd muttered when Tristan gave him the knife, are always inefficient. But he accepted it gracefully, otherwise.

Down through the plaza, a group of Maestros, three women, a man, and Father Dolan, sang something in Yaqui from sheets of paper. Tristan wished Refugio were here to translate. They'd sing the whole song, then advance a few steps. Behind them, lines and lines of Fariseos and Chapayekas inched forward as well, slapping swords against sticks in a rhythm, rattling their rattles, raising dust, threatening with their spears. They advanced toward a line of gray ash.

Tristan smelled the *carne seca,* and something else—soap, maybe. He looked at this ceremony, inching forward. These Yaqui. Their demeanor was a careless sidling up to all the most important things in life. Not content to adapt American customs, and not being able to afford them, they fashioned their lives with a roll-your-own aspect that left a Westerner like Tristan, a faggot like Tristan, wanting to perfect things. The jury-rigged nature of Yaqui life dissatisfied him viscerally.

The Maestros, and all of the files behind them, moved glacially, absorbed the crowd like an amoeba surrounding its food. Four days of this, nonstop! Because there was time for it, everything was done properly. Nobody seemed to be leading, nobody was in charge. There was the priest, but Father Dolan looked like he was being pulled along, and ought not to have been there, since this was some major heresy.

Suddenly, on some secret signal, there was a charge by the embattled forces of darkness against light. Bells in the church began to ring wildly. Tristan could see two men pulling on the rope from within the church.

Men in masks and robes charged in step from one end of the plaza, up to the ramada, and were rebuffed to the other, down to the place where the effigy of Judas stood. As they ran back and forth, people in the crowd broke open their cascarones or revealed big bags of confetti, which they threw in the air. The sky was suddenly brilliant with bright colored bits of paper, shiny stars, crepe rolls, and it fell the way the rain should have fallen from the *verga* clouds. It was beautiful. But Tristan didn't crack open his egg.

When everything calmed down, the Fariseos and Chapayekas reformed their lines, though advanced, behind the Maestros and the priest, who had held their ground during the battle.

Tristan finally pointed out Father Dolan. "That was the priest that said mass for Joe's funeral."

Mik nodded. "I know. Do you know what happened to him after the funeral?"

"Something happened to him?"

"He had to go to a clinic for a few months, because he'd become an alcoholic. Drank himself into a stupor. He was lucky they gave him this post in the Yaqui village."

"Huh," Tristan said, which he tried to make sound uninterested. "I wonder what the padre thinks of all these heretical numbers. I wonder what he thinks of boys in skirts. I wonder what he thinks of Jesús Malverde and all the other unofficial saints." Like Joe.

"You mean the Church doesn't approve?"

"The Pope hasn't approved of them. Some of them aren't saints, they're just soul intercessors. In the right place and time, Joe would be a victim intercessor."

Mik said, "What's the difference?"

"They don't even pretend that some of these guys are saints. Some are just *alma,* soul. Like Pedro Blanco." Pedro Blanco won big gambling one evening in the 1920s. As he walked home alone, he was robbed and killed in the night. He was buried where he fell, and a small chapel was erected and he began answering prayers and granting miracles. "But he's fallen out of fashion," Tristan told Mik. "He lost his powers over the years, and his shrine isn't even kept clean any more. People of the drug trade pray to the devil if they need the sort of help that only the devil will provide. But once their rivals have been rubbed out or the big shipment of dope has gone through, they don't repay the devil but God, the Virgin, and the saints."

"So it's just superstition."

"Isn't that all we've got left, religionwise?" Tristan really wanted to know. "These people see Jesus in a forkful of spaghetti and the Blessed Virgin in their fireplace soot. Mik, I have to say, I'm jealous."

Just then, the second battle whooshed into motion. Those bells were insistent, portentous. The confetti roiled. Tristan could have sworn it made the heat waves visible.

Suddenly, his nose was bleeding. It had been bleeding a little when he blew the dust out in the evenings, from being in high dry country. Now it dripped down to his lip and he tasted it, metallic and tainted. He was breathing it, too. He had that feeling he'd had when he ran very fast over a long distance, raw lungs, steely air. Mik saw the blood and offered a hanky. Tristan refused it. He had a napkin.

"It's so dry," he explained.

"Your body adapts," Mik said.

The forces of darkness had regrouped for one last charge. The Maestros sang loudly. There was an actual tension this time. The armies inched forward, rattling and stalking.

This time, everybody was throwing all of their confetti. The bells, no longer portentous, now rang joyfully from the church. And this time, the Fariseos and their minions lost. As each Chapayeka was defeated, his mask was removed, tossed onto the pile of wood beneath the Judas effigy. One by one, their costumes were taken from them, their swords and sticks and blankets. Good riddance, Tristan thought, thinking of the way they'd treated Maria.

Then something happened that surprised Tristan. Out of the crowd, dozens and dozens of women came running into the battle. They fought through waves of confetti and cheers and drums and whistles, and over the shoulders of each vanquished Chapayeka, they threw a beautiful woven blanket. They held the stripped-down men close to them, and hustled them into the church, brought them before the Three Marys and the crucifix and fell to their knees in a huddle.

"These women are their godmothers," Mik explained. "They're rededicating themselves to Christ and the Church." He reached over and broke the egg on Tristan's cascarone. "Participate," he said.

Tristan shook confetti out onto the plaza like everybody else. He poured some onto his own head. It was flying up into the air. Somewhere hidden by daylight was the comet. Everything was in the air somewhere, with the bits of paper: stars and unraining clouds, dust devils and Hale-Bopp. Even the huge billboard with its glittery jackpot numbers was some kind of secret sign.

Two, three at a time, the lost bad men were hustled, embraced, even kissed by these women as they crossed the long plaza. Oh, to be held so tight and loved so much, and to be saved, to be rededi-cated to something, Tristan thought. The woman who'd had the unused disposable diaper had dropped her sunblock and carried a blanket out for one of the last fallen clown warriors, the one who'd been dressed as a Chinaman. He was throwing his mask onto the bonfire, which had just been lit. The woman threw her blanket around his sweating shoulders, and turned him around so that he could see the church and Tristan could see his face for the first time. He was a boy, not much older than Refugio.

Tristan began to cry, just as the firecrackers began to make his ears ring with the thunder of battle. The cheers, the bells, the confetti, the hustling, the holding, the singing. A home, a return.

14

Tristan pulled from his pocket a picture he'd had for years. It was a prayer card, a picture of Jesús Malverde on a prayer card. It was the image of a handsome young man dressed in a light-colored shirt with dark pocket flaps.

Mik had just dropped him off so he could rest up, take a shower, see Mrs. Jimenez before he went over to Maria's for dinner. He'd been out in the heat for so long, the adobe B and B felt like a refrigerator. He went to the sink and drew a glass of water.

And now Tristan had just broken a glass, a good one. He had an annoyingly insurmountable habit of placing breakable objects at the precarious edges of counters, ledges, and shelves for easy access. He'd been shaking out his pills again, all the varieties, the protease with the D4T with the 3TC, as well as a multivitamin and a vitamin C with rosehips. He spilled out a handful onto the kitchen table and as sometimes happened, the exact regimen of three blues, one white, one red, and two yellows skittered to rest. "Yahtzee!" Tristan shouted on these rare occasions, and celebrated it by bringing up his hands in a victory flex. The glass went over onto the cement floor.

Now he was sweeping up the shards and wondering whether to tell Mrs. Jimenez about it in the morning, or to hide the evidence. He'd already broken that glass by the pool. He placed the shards in a paper bag and then put the bag in his suitcase. What benefit would there be in disappointing her?

"I think I need to get my eyes checked," he had said to Mik earlier in the day, when he'd spilled once again, coffee, all down the front of his shirt. It was a long dribble that would never wash out. Red wine, buttery sauces, anything permanent—he managed to inflict it on his clothes. Ties with solid colors were coming back into fashion; Tristan had seen the portents in fine men's clothiers and he had despaired.

Mik had watched him and shook his head. Did Mik think it was possible, Tristan wondered, that trouble with eye-hand coordination could affect your whole life? Could bad eyesight lead to bad insight? He felt like asking Mik about this, but he was afraid Mik might figure him out.

After hiding the glass, Tristan looked down at his pharmaceutical good-and-plenty handful: "Better living through chemistry," he said out loud, and bombs away.

The bed was big and comfortable, especially for one. He could hear the springs ping under his weight. He looked down under the cotton sheets—she'd come in and changed the linens after one night!—and saw rivulets of purple webbing on one side of both knees. "Varicose veins," he marveled. I am old, I am old, I shall wear my trousers rolled.

Was it this room or the one next to it where Joe and Tristan had stayed the last time Joe was well enough to make the trip? Joe had been winding down, sleeping a lot and worrying. They were watching television in the bedroom and Tristan had slapped down to the bathroom barefoot. With his pants around his ankles and his mind someplace else, it took him a beat or two to understand the shadow of the scorpion behind the garbage can. Tristan shot up, shuffling out clown-style with his pants in a bind, shrieking an interesting string of swear words that had never come out quite that way before: "Jesus fuck oh my fucking god damn shit shit shit!" Something like that.

Tristan fell on the bed where Joe lay absorbed in television. "It's the biggest, oh Joe—scorpion—I can't begin to tell you!"

This would have gone on much longer had Joe been able to hide his grin—yes, he was a saint, he couldn't bear for it to go on—he cracked up and Tristan suddenly understood that it was a rubber scorpion.

"Ha, ha, ha," Tristan said, smacking Joe in the thigh, the same place where Kaposi's sarcoma was beginning to stain the flesh. "People die of heart attacks, too." The joke worked a second time, the next day, when Tristan found the toy planted by the drain in the ill-lit shower stall.

But nature, red in tooth and claw, was why Joe had brought him to Sonora in the spring, when barrel cacti bloom. Tristan would carry around his *Audubon Society Guide to Deserts* and identify them all, teddybear chollas and the arrow weed, jojoba, ocotillo, smoke tree, saguaro, yucca, tamarisk, palo verde, mesquite, crucifixion thorn, elephant tree, Mormon tea, turpentine broom. Stingy most of the year, then spendthrift with a flower born of poverty and too-much/too-fast rainfall, that was the desert for Tristan, prickly, poisoned, austere, and suddenly decadent. Oh, the ocotillo, lit in epiphanical flames of flowers! Prairie dogs, lizards, hummingbirds, the bee assassin and the Jerusalem cricket, the marooned tortoise, nightjars, and owls.

This was his fifth visit to Sonora. Now he came with open arms to this desolate place, marveled that the kangaroo rats peed crystals of urine to retain water, and that the brown recluse spider's poison ate flesh. Nature made no pretense of kindness here; there'd be no dreams of a scorpion's embrace.

Tristan wondered: Tricky Joe, how had you made me love to sleep with scorpions? Joe was not exactly a moral creature but a man who surrounded himself with moral friends, a kind of moral brain trust. But Tristan was as clumsy morally as he was with objects. It wasn't that he waffled, but that, sensualist as he was, he could see the benefit of vice. Ill-gotten gains, selfish pleasure, something for nothing. It was his imagination that revved slowly, like a lawn mower that didn't start up easily on its pull cord. When it did get going, it operated beautifully, but often Tristan was burned. Any number of disappointed sleazeballs got to Tristan's doorstep, only to have the door frantically shut in their faces. Tristan could hear them on the other side, cursing and threatening.

"It's like I see a piece of cheese in the mousetrap," he once explained to Joe after a particularly clumsy occasion, when he'd almost signed a contract with a fly-by-night correspondence course instructorship, and returned the contract, so carefully tailored to his wishes, unsigned, and received an unenforceable letter full of anger and requests to pay for the cost of all that contractual work. "I reach for the cheese and then I see the trap in my fingers' futures. Just as I touch the cheese, I realize my danger and pull away, but the trap is sprung." No cheese, and lots of pain.

Mik would never do that, Tristan decided. Mik probably thought about morality all the time and took pleasure in an arid desert of nonsensual rewards, another kind of sin not worth going into—but never with a mousetrap involved.

Tristan was reading in a book of Sonoran history, and, as usual, he gravitated to the myths and legends. Here, he found another of the victim intercessors, Tita Gómez. She was on a hill with what she thought was her true-blue boyfriend picking wild onions. She was murdered with a tire iron by the boyfriend and his wife, and buried where she fell. Her grave became a place of petitions. Tristan looked up from the book.

"How are your parents?" Mrs. Jimenez asked.

They were killing a few minutes, waiting for Mik to pick him up for dinner at Maria's. He was sitting in her living room drinking iced tea.

They were distracted, craning their necks out the window looking for the familiar car. A tow truck drove by hauling away a behemoth Cadillac. Its complicated alarm, a drunken blaring toodle, was going off in protest, as if the tow truck were a pirate and the Cadillac a buxom wench.

She always asked about his family in her bimonthly phone calls. They exchanged Christmas cards. Of this, he was informed by both parties.

"Well, I'm afraid my grandmother has died."

"Oh dear," she said, "I'm so sorry."

You shouldn't be, he thought to himself. She was a horrid bigoted bitch; she would have called you a dirty spic even though your family has been in this country longer than mine, and she never was going to change—only death could change a person like that. But he said, "I don't want to sound unkind, but when somebody dies when they're old, I feel like it's right. Appropriate."

He was sometimes sorry to be so nice with Mrs. Jimenez, and thought a lot could be gained by their being more honest with each other. But their history together was a long Silly Slide of mutual comfort, and the inertia of that could not be halted. The broken glass remained hidden in his suitcase.

"And The Boys? Do you ever see The Boys?"

"The Boys" were a half-dozen of Joe's friends. Tristan had never had any real difficulty with any of them except that they struck him as slightly lame. Charles was a honey-throated fat old guy who'd spent the entire relationship between Joe and Tristan unemployed and unattached. Under the guise of heartbrokenness, Charles wished for Joe's love. Tristan had never been jealous—Joe was gorgeous, his beauty another thing he'd been too generous with. He was the kind of handsome man who never believed in his own handsomeness.

The Boys pissed Tristan off, though, in the last days. Charles's unemployment made him ubiquitous, prone to melodramatic deathbed scenes involving warm washcloths on the brow and swansong arias on the stereo. Donald hired a friend of a friend who was a chiropractor to make five perfunctory, five-minute adjustments, and expected Tristan to pay a tip. Larry the speed queen would promise to bring Joe a hot lunch, and then pick up a boy somewhere and never show up. Tristan would come home from a long day at work and find a long night of it to come—caring more for Joe's friends than Joe himself—cooking, cleaning up, entertaining.

Oh, why lie? He didn't like those guys, and when he least wanted to see them, they were always there.

And they had their little conspiratorial hatreds of him, too. That Tristan did not have or drive a car was a constant threat to Joe's well-being. That Charles's church loaned them a washing machine was constantly lorded over him. And the thing never did work. And, of course, there was the quilt panel issue.

Then, in the end, when Joe slipped away and Mrs. Jimenez was staying in the house for four days while waiting for Joe's ashes and plane tickets and paperwork, Charles befriended Mrs. Jimenez when Tristan himself had no strength or wish to console her. She loved Charles. Tristan had wished Charles would sink into the earth.

It didn't take long for any of them to go their separate ways.

"Not Chris? Not Conrad? Not Chow-Chow? Not Charles?"

Tristan shrugged, embarrassed. "I get so busy, you know? And I think a couple of them have moved away."

"They haven't died, have they? It would be so terrible if they've died."

The Boys: Conrad, that drunkard. Chris, the disco bunny. And Chow-Chow, ugh. Given the name because he supposedly had a fried blond hairdo that poofed out in all directions, and made him look like an exotic show dog. It wasn't worth explaining to Mrs. Jimenez that Tristan had never even met Chow-Chow in the flesh. He was too much of a flake to come to the house (and yet he'd somehow become in Tristan's mind the quintessential dumb blond). Sometimes, in Tristan's meaner moods, he wondered whether Joe surrounded himself with these leaden jerks to make himself seem lighter, kinder, more magical and generous, the way a plain bride would choose uglier bridesmaids.

"No, I'm sure they're all just fine." Looking after themselves, he thought. Only the good die young.

"What's it like to be old?" he suddenly asked her, and realized once again he'd said the wrong thing. A dundering fool rushing in, but if he was careless, nobody could say he wasn't enthusiastic. He really wanted to know.

She sharpened herself, then he saw her face smooth over, perhaps recognizing the enthusiasm, and spoke as an innkeeper, a thing she could always fall back on. "You start keeping track of your family more, where everybody is placewise, you can't force them to be near you. . . . " She trailed off, and it wasn't melodrama; she did get distracted by her own unexpected meanings. "But you can say, I want you to visit me for Easter, and you offer to pay the plane ticket."

So Tristan was family. "I would have come and paid my own way." He was feeling less beholden, the chafing over the insurance payoff had begun to grow stronger. She should fly him around the damn world, as a matter of fact.

15

"And now it's time for *Ask Mister Wizard!* With the star of our show, the man who knows it all and then some, Mister Wizard, Uncle Mik!" Maria had a salt shaker to her mouth. Earl was handling the video camera and kept stone silent.

They'd put the kids' play desk at Mik's disposal. It had big, fat, colored magnetic letters across the top spelling the name of the show. Mik was wearing white, a Meccan white. He had his luxurious hair done up in a goofy pony tail that shot straight from the top of his head. The chair that both Maria and Tristan liked was for Tristan, the very special guest on *Ask Mister Wizard.*

"Tonight," Mik said sincerely to the camera, "I have two of my favorite contestants. Will you please welcome, ladies and gentlemen, Captain Twitch"—this was Maria's oldest son—"and Señor Blahblah." Señor Blahblah, despite being six, had a pacifier in his mouth. "And later on in the show, we've got a special treat, that old friend of Uncle Joe's, Tristan Broder."

"Hey, Monkey!" Maria called out. It sounded very stale.

Mik was so earnest. The kids just loved that.

"But first, a word from our sponsor." Mik put out a hand. The kids knew exactly what to do. They'd been taping *Ask Mister Wizard* for a couple of years now. Maria once sent Tristan a tape with several episodes, after Tristan had sent her a tape of his and Joe's domestic partnership, a vacation to New Orleans, and the memorial service, all on one cassette.

Earl brought his camera around to the side. Maria and her kids had props in their hands, and on "3," sang a song that was half jingle, half hymn: "Marshmallow Peeps and froggy legs/Easter

Bunny's Easter eggs/Jesus loves me this I know/You can make it with Play-Doh."

General applause. Froggy legs?

"And back to our program. Tell me, Señor Blahblah, have you got a question for Mister Wizard?"

Señor Blahblah had been so nicknamed four years ago, when he learned to talk long before other kids his age, but usually babbled endlessly about nothing to himself, or repeated a sentence some adult had said, over and over: "Eat your corn eat your corn eat your corn."

While Señor Blahblah (what was the kid's real name?) continued building his before-its-time vocabulary and also excelled at math problems, there were still baby toys and baby food. And yet—and yet, he was perfectly articulate, having learned how to enunciate clearly around the mouth barrier in order to be understood. Tristan was reminded of that ancient Greek orator—Teiresius? Thucydides?—who practiced talking with his mouth full of pebbles in order to ready himself for important speeches.

Señor Blahblah, pleased to Ask Mister Wizard first, looked like a ventriloquist when his question came out.

"In my classroom? On the bulletin board? It said March comes in like a lion and out like a lamb? And Mrs. Cicero took it down so she could put up the Easter bunny?"

"Yes?" Mik, like Tristan, was trying to figure out what the question was.

"And all the colored paper that was behind the letters and the lion and the lamb was darker and you could still read where the letters were."

"Oh, sure," said Mik. "That's because the sun bleached the paper."

"That's what Mom said."

"And so what would you like Mister Wizard to tell you?"

"Where does the color go when the sun bleaches it?"

That, Tristan thought, was a good question. But Mik was ever The Great Explainer, and described what happened to color and satisfied Señor Blahblah, and Tristan, for that matter.

"How about a question from Captain Twitch?"

Captain Twitch, who was about one year away from being too cool for *Ask Mister Wizard,* got his name from his ongoing inability to sit still. His question was more scientific: he wanted to know how a refrigerator made things cold. Mik was able to describe freon and tubes and once again, Tristan was enlightened. He had a revelation: Mik was smarter than he was.

"Today we are going to learn some more about maps." Mister Wizard had pinned a series of charts onto the wall. "Here is a picture of the Yaqui reservation, Pascua." He pointed with a billiard cue from Earl's rec room to a map of Tucson and vicinity. "There are three Yaqui settlements in this area; the second is in the south part of town, called Libre. There is a third one, near San Xavier de Bac, called New Pascua. The first was created by a Yaqui man named Pistola. The village was given to the tribe and then a real estate company parceled off the land for houses."

Mister Wizard tore this map off the wall. Now there was a map of Africa. "Can you see the lines for all of the different countries?" He was pointing to sharp straight lines that divided rivers, cultures, and natural resources. "Can you guess who drew these borders? Do you think it was the Africans?" Then Mister Wizard laughed. He pulled an imaginary tobacco pipe to his mouth and did his best imitation of a stodgy, arrogant British cartographer. "Old chap, just draw the line here and here, righto!" The absurdity of this made everybody laugh, even the boys, even though they might not completely understand it.

He revealed a third and final map, this of India and neighboring Pakistan. "And who do you think drew these borders? And who made all those people who were Muslim leave the country so that India could be a Hindu country? Somebody draws a line, and everybody has to move. That's how it works. End of lesson."

There were no questions from the studio audience. Earl went up to the map and swept over India's regions with his camera. Mister Wizard pointed to the Punjab region. Maria hollered, "Hey, Monkey!"

This time, Tristan looked significantly toward Maria. But he did not say, "Cut it out."

Mister Wizard turned to Tristan. "How about you, Tristan Broder, our special guest? Do you have a question for Mister Wizard?"

Tristan had a million questions. There were mischievous ones that might piss off Maria and Earl. Where do babies come from? Why do some boys like boys instead of girls? Is there really an Easter Bunny? There were more pressing ones: Is there a God? You who do not have enchanted legs, what are you looking for? Why am I still alive? But he decided to take advantage of Mister Wizard's skill. He asked, "Why do some people think that it's perfectly okay to eat a pizza with ham and pineapple on it?"

"Oh, wow," said Maria, "I have always thought that that was a disgusting combination."

"You two," Earl said, turning the camera off for a second.

And when he set it rolling again, Mik said, "Since Mister Wizard does not eat meat, he must excuse himself from the question concerning ham."

Now it was Tristan's turn to answer some questions. "Señor Blahblah and Captain Twitch have not seen Uncle Joe in a long time, and sometimes it's hard for them to remember him. Perhaps you can tell us a little bit about Uncle Joe?"

Earl's camera was right up in his face. Tristan didn't know what to say. "Well, Señor, Captain, sometimes it's hard for me to remember him, too." Maria exaggerated a puzzled expression. "I mean, sometimes it's easier to see all the things he always had around him, you know? That beat-up van he had to carry his tools in, he named it Thumper, after the bunny in *Bambi*. His cheap gray sweatshirts. *Star Trek*. Do you ever watch *Star Trek*? Uncle Joe loved *Star Trek*. And fried chicken. And going to the beach. And stand-up comedians."

Captain Twitch said, "When we pray to him, should we tell him jokes?"

A panda walks into a bar.

"Only if they're funny and not dirty." Did they pray to him? Tristan only wrote letters. And didn't Pentecostals dismiss the pantheon of angels and saints? "Uncle Joe could swallow big things because he had a big mouth. Did you know that? If you had a big handful of vitamins and pills, maybe twelve, he could gulp them down in one bite."

"Wow," said Señor Blahblah from behind the pacifier.

"But don't you try doing that," said Maria.

Tristan said, "Right. Uncle Joe could do it because he was a magician. He could do amazing things with electricity and plants. When he got sick, he needed to make a special no-barf potion from a special plant you can't get at the nursery. So he built a special secret garden in the garage with pretty violet lights and pretty silver foil all around these big plants that smelled like a faraway land, or an Italian restaurant. When the plants grew up, he would dry the leaves of the magic plant —"

"Dinnertime!" Earl chimed as he dropped the camera. Just like that, *Ask Mister Wizard* was over. The boys clambered up the stairs. Earl was right behind them, leaving Mik and Maria and Tristan a perfect triangle of surprise.

"I'm sorry," said Tristan. "I don't know what I was thinking."

"Joe grew pot?" Mik looked like he'd just found out his best friend had been a werewolf all these years.

"Well, of course. Haven't you been watching the news? It's medicinal. It keeps you from barfing all the time. Believe me, he was entitled to it. There was fluid in his lungs and fluid on his brain and whatever. Do you think a human being can take all that?" He looked over at Maria. "Earl is pissed, isn't he?"

"Well, I think it was because of the kids. He doesn't think kids need to know about magical mystery tour plants. Let's go eat."

Upstairs, Earl's father was wedged into a chair at one end of the table and the two boys were helping him cut up his food. Earl had cooked. His specialty was pancakes. Tristan liked the idea of pancakes for dinner.

On each of the plates were two or three silver-dollar-sized flapjacks. There were sausages and fruit salad, too. Nothing but breakfast in Tucson!

"Aren't you going to eat with us?" Tristan asked when Earl didn't sit down.

"No, Boss, I'm the chef." He avoided looking directly at Tristan. Yes, he was pissed. But he led them in grace and bustled in and out of the kitchen bringing more and more pancakes.

Only Tristan was drinking, he realized, already pouring a second big glass of wine. The one least fit for snorting up poison. When he drank too much he sometimes got diarrhea, and he knew that his liver was chugging away like an overworked steam engine. That was how he would die.

What was it with temperance people serving alcohol for the sake of their guests? The secretary for City College's English department was a known anorexic, and three days out of five, she'd set out huge pans of brownies or coffee cake she'd baked the night before; she'd hover over it while you took a wedge, and watch you eat it. The look upward, which said, "Heaven!" while your mouth was crammed with crumbs, whether you meant it or not, made her day, and was all the sustenance she apparently needed.

Maria and Mik watched him quaff, so Tristan exaggerated his gusto once more.

Tristan ate a lot, too, and the pancakes soaked up grease and syrup and wine and milk and juice and the dough expanded in his stomach. When Joe and he were partnered at city hall, their friends threw Rice-A-Roni at them as they left, and the cabbie they hailed yelled at them, for everybody knew pigeons ate that stuff and it blew up in their stomachs until the pigeons died. "I hate pigeons," Tristan had said, selfishly and destructively happy in the heat of that moment, and Joe thought it was the naughtiest thing Tristan had ever said.

Nobody talked during dinner, but Earl's father muttered for things and people seemed to know what he was requesting. Two or three times, conversations might have gotten started, but nobody had the energy to follow up. Mik had talked about maps and borders, evidently, in order to talk about land and land use. He told Tristan later that he was always trying to slip ideas into the boys' heads. "Some slip in better then others."

Tristan thought he ought to feel bad for making Earl so angry, but instead, he kept thinking about what it must be like to see Maria the Pentecostal ranting and raving in some jump-and-shout church downtown. Or maybe Pentecostals were more reserved these days. As much as he wanted to torture Catholic priests with his brazen poofterisms, his snobbery (the same snobbery that made him want to go into the Yaqui village like a big fag town talent show director and really dazzle the little people, cover the place with real flowers, stage a couple of Chapayeka skits and do it right and fabulously, goddammit) made him think that Pentecostalism was a step down, a marriage beneath her. After so much sophistication, ritual, elaborate training, she'd turned to snake handling and fainting. It was so uncouth, Tristan decided, but knew that sort of thinking wasn't quite right.

"I was thinking of going to see the Matachini maypole dance," said Tristan. "Anybody interested in going with me?"

Earl breezed out. "We've decided we hate the Yaqui and all they stand for, haven't we, Maria?" Earl had been acting downright queenly this evening—serving dinner, gathering in his skirts—for a guy who had mudflap girls on his truck.

Maria looked like she wouldn't have put it exactly that way, but they all knew she didn't have a chip to bargain with. Being raped by Chapayekas was just too much.

"How about you, Mik?"

Mik sat up straight. His hair was still done in that idiotic fountain. "I'm sorry, Tristan. This is my night for worship. But I promise to go with you to the Easter Sunday ceremonies tomorrow morning."

"What's the big deal?" Tristan tried to joke. "I thought Saturday was supposed to be downtime for most of Western Religion? Why all this activity today? Isn't this when Jesus is sleeping?"

"He isn't sleeping," said Captain Twitch, "he's resurrecting."

Maria put a hand on her son's hand. "Maybe you can borrow my mom's car to drive there yourself. I'm sure she'll let you. Here, let me call. Then we'll drive you over to her house."

She looked at him with that look. The one of Recognition. The one she gave him the day they'd been in the auto graveyard and she opened up their society of two. Here was its matching bookend, the eyes straight on.

They couldn't wait to get rid of him.

16

Mrs. Jimenez had the car of a woman whose life was in control. It was not extravagant but seemed plush by being a dusty gold color. There were fleece seat covers and she had two matching round gold windshield shades that said "Help Call Police" on the inside, and Tristan jumped a little at it before he realized what it was for. There was a smart black oven mitt in the passenger seat for opening the car door in blazing sun.

Mrs. Jimenez advised Tristan to get gas if he saw it anywhere for less than a buck-forty-one a gallon, even though the tank was two-thirds full. "I'll reimburse you," she said, which was a false offer, and Tristan stored away the important errand of filling the tank with gas at whatever price.

The dashboard had three glued-down figurines of Jesus, Mary, and a Sacred Heart Auto League symbol. A little laminated playing-card-sized placard, framed with spines, read, " 'How much do you love me?' I asked Jesus, and Jesus said, 'This much.' Then he spread his arms and died for me."

The radio was tuned to a light rock station, which alternated love songs with lost love songs. This stuff, besides being the ongoing atrocity of pop, made Tristan envious. Love songs were painfully simple. There were no love songs, lost or otherwise, that could convey his own amorous history. He tried to make one up: "Oh baby, I was so hurt when you left me for that disease, I got so damn depressed I went out and got my own disease, but your mother thinks I'm still holding a torch for you but I don't, I don't, I don't."

Let's face it, he thought, what I have is not romantic. Whatever had been said about illness as a metaphor didn't cover the fact that if Joe had died of tuberculosis they'd have written operas about him. Even cancer merited a bloated television movie. There would be no operas about AIDS, let alone protease inhibitors. Well, actually, there *were* operas, but they were dreadful things, best left unheard.

"I grow old, I grow old, I shall wear my trousers rolled," Tristan said out loud, even though he was alone, as he stepped out of the car and among a group of boys and girls smoking dope, swooping around on rollerblades. They were loitering and Tristan had to step carefully if he didn't want to bump into them as they swooped. They could pass off their little swoops as accidents, but truly their recklessness was all on purpose; he turned back and saw them do the same thing to a lady.

It was a regular loitering place out in front of somebody's adobe, judging from the hard-packed earth in what was ostensibly the front yard and the kind of trash that lay all around—tiny trash, gum wrappers, bits of garbage bag skewered on dried weeds, a crushed tin can. In the window of the adobe was a sign written in magic marker on the back of shoebox cardboard: "Just Be Peaceful."

"Hey, *panzón!*" yelled one of the rollerbladers, and Tristan realized they were talking to him, caught him looking back, caught him giving them the time of day. "Does your girlfriend got big titties?"

Tristan was confused. He didn't have a girlfriend; he didn't like big titties. And *"panzón"*? The big belly? Was he so fat that strangers would call him that? Or was none of this to be taken personally?

Tristan liked the confusion. Being here without Mik and Maria felt liberating and he saw the village for the first time with his old lascivious eyes. He enjoyed the bad boy asking him, *panzón*, whether his girlfriend had big titties. He walked back to the rollerbladers.

"Do you know Jesús Malverde?" he asked.

"Does he go to Old Pascua school, or the church school, *panzón?*" This one was probably the leader: whippet-wiry, the darting eyes of a lookout guard, big, clumsy troublesome hands.

Tristan smiled. "He's the patron saint of bad boys."

Whippet Boy sneered, but it was clearly a badge of honor to be associated with the patron he didn't know he had. "Oh sure, him. But, you know, we got our own, man. He's one of the regular guys. We got a special one."

Tristan smiled and waved good-bye. They all smiled and waved back. Tristan shifted his waving to two firemen spending most of their firewatch keeping an eye on the bad boys. They leaned against their truck and waved back.

Tristan thought one of them was gorgeous, half Yaqui and half something else. He had a widow's peak so pronounced that Tristan had to decide whether it was icky or hot. That he had to decide, then, made it hotter.

There were two boys in a scruffy little plane tree, trying to see the ceremony and trying to escape the dust being kicked up by the Matachinis. What was the name of that man in the tree in the Bible? Started with a Z. Zachariah? Zebadiah?

"Want to buy a rosary?" said a girl with a wide, piggy nose. She had a bag full of the special Yaqui *rosarios* made of pea-sized carved wooden beads in a bracelet-sized loop on the end of a long string, to be worn around the neck. It ended in a cross with a tassle of blue or pink feathers. They called anything fearlessly, boldly colored a "flower." And flowers had power. The masks of the Chapayekas were called flowers. Flowers killed them in La Gloria. Mrs. Jimenez's Christmas-colored B and B would be a flower in Yaqui-ville. The Fariseos, Mik had explained, were killed by flowers in the afternoon battle of La Gloria.

Tristan gave her a five-dollar bill. He turned around, and there he was, his quarry, the secret goal of the entire evening. And the night was young. The sun was setting and the dust was clearing and the heat was abating. Tristan had all night for this.

"Hello, Father."

"Hello."

"Then you remember me."

"Of course I remember you. And you remember me."

"Very well. We're a memorable couple of guys."

"Lion in Winter."

"What?"

"That's a takeoff from *The Lion in Winter*. The line is actually, 'We're a knowledgeable family.' "

Not a good way to start the attack: so far, Tristan had been outgayed, hadn't known his *Lion in Winter*. Parry, thrust. "Well, what do you think of all this, Father?"

"All of what?" A Caballero walked out of the ramada. From his neck hung one of the Yaqui *rosarios,* this one with a red tassle. Was red for boys and blue for girls? Had Tristan bought the wrong one? Under the arbor of the ramada, there was a little statue of the baby Jesus, a corner of his nose slightly chipped (nothing a little makeup wouldn't fix), and several women were hanging more paper flowers.

"What do you think of these rosaries, for instance?" he asked the priest. "Hard to keep track of your Our Fathers and Hail Marys with this one."

Father Dolan seemed to get less nervous rather than more. He twisted the ring on his pinky, but then he stopped. He shook some confetti out of his collar. Tristan would later find even more confetti in the pouch of his underwear, and when he washed his hair in the shower, three paper-punch-sized stains, red, purple, and green, would stay in the white porcelain even after he took a scrubbie to them.

"So what can I do for you, Tristan?" He even remembered Tristan's name. "I saw you were quite moved by La Gloria."

The priest had seen Tristan cry. Retreat, retreat. "It was something," Tristan said.

Refugio was suddenly there, an apparition. "You came," he said. "Where's Mik?"

"He couldn't make it. He said to tell you personally that he was sorry about that and he'd make it up to you."

"Hello, Refugio," said Father Dolan.

Refugio saluted the priest. They were excellent friends.

"Hey, Refugio!" One of the boys called from the plane tree. "When is the maypole?"

Refugio looked up into the tree. "As soon as I pee."

Tristan realized that Refugio hadn't just appeared, nor was he following Tristan around. He was in line to use the one available public Porta Potti, and he was mincing around with his knees together in order to hold it in. Two of the loitering bad kids, including Whippet Boy, cut in front of Refugio, sliced in front of him, actually, on their rollerblades. When they saw the way Refugio was dancing around, they started making fun of the pudding-faced Matachini. *"Chupa, chupa,"* Whippet said.

"Chupacabra!" the second one said, and Whippet thought this was simply hilarious, even though it wasn't. It was a kind of dunderhead humor, Tristan believed, that made it a remarkable thing that the world could barely go on turning. All the boy had done was turn "suck, suck" into "goatsucker." Goatsucker, *Chupacabra,* was the latest mythical creature of the region, some green, big-eyed monster that drank the blood of goats. Like an unofficial saint, *Chupacabra* was adored by the masses, and Tristan had considered buying T-shirts with the creature's likeness for Maria's boys.

Somebody left the Porta Potti and the two rollerbladed bullies entered together. Typical. When Tristan was in high school and actually dated girls, he'd run into the troublemakers at the mall, six boys at a time, who'd sit behind Tristan and his girl at the movies and say, "Hey faggot, suck me, faggot," mostly because that particular girl wouldn't go out with any of them and also because Tristan could type fast, etcetera. "Hey faggot, what's your boyfriend going to say when he finds out you're with some chick?" They'd go on and on, spoiling the movie and never realizing how ironic it was that Tristan was rubbing thighs with a girl while they sat behind, rubbing thighs with each other in the dark.

"They're probably gonna smoke weed," Refugio said. "This will take forever."

Even though he was the object of disdain, Tristan felt strangely comfortable with these traditional roles: bully, fag, closeted terrified priest. It puzzled him to cope in a land of accepted fags, confident priests.

Tristan turned to Father Dolan again. He was dying to ask how old the priest was. "What made you decide to become pastor of the Yaqui village church?"

"Saint Ygnacio," said Father Dolan.

"Is he an offical saint?"

"Oh, who cares? It's perfect for a priest who needs to keep busy. Did you know that almost half the days of the year are ceremonial days here?"

Refugio was the only one waiting for the toilet, so he came over to them, half overhearing their conversation. "Do you know how Mary remained a Virgin?" Refugio said it to both of the white men. "She smelled a flower, and that's how Jesus was born. Mary should always have flowers near her." He pointed to his own ornate headdress. "When they were getting ready to crucify Jesus, they went to Joseph because he was such a good carpenter. 'Make a cross so we can put your son on it.' But all the wood was too short. Then Jesus came up to Joseph and said he was God, and if Joseph would just go out in the hills, he would find a tree big enough. Then Joseph just stood there, because he couldn't believe it. But after a while, he went out in the desert and he found a tree and he chopped it down. But the tree was really Mary; she'd turned herself into a tree. This was the big plan. Jesus, God, and Mary had talked it over. So when Jesus got crucified he was crucified on a cross that was really his mother. Her arms are stretched out like this, just like a mother's should be, to embrace her son."

Nobody was coming out of the toilet. Tristan thought the boys were getting completely baked in that closed space, inhaling tokes and breathing in the exhaled fumes. But there wasn't even any pot smoke leaking out of the air vents.

"Is that true?" Tristan asked Father Dolan.

"More or less."

Had Tristan misjudged this man as a coward?

"I've really got to go," said Refugio.

The Pascolas and the Deer Dancer were leading the fiesta. No more the strike of sword and dagger making rhythms. This was all water drums and flutes. The Fariseos, all dressed in black like gangsters, were gone. The world was a gentle place again, growing more simplified in the Resurrection.

Father Dolan strode to the Porta Potti and rapped three times. Tristan thought of that Catholic image of Jesus knocking on a door, the door of the heart of a human. Why didn't some transgressive San Francisco artist do a picture of Jesus knocking on a Porta Potti door: "I've really got to go."

Father Dolan said, "Boys, you're holding everybody up out here." No sound. "Boys, come out of there."

"They're doing it because I'm gay," said Refugio.

Father Dolan said, "They're doing it to get attention."

Tristan looked around. All over the village, the Stations of the Cross had been "awakened." They stood once again. His little guidebook promised an all-night fiesta. While Dolan yelled at the locked-up toilet, Refugio, doubled-over, took a moment to translate the Deer Dancer song for Tristan. "Do you hear this? It's my favorite song. It says, 'But there in heaven, truly it is as if enchanted, my father.' "

"Boys, do I have to get somebody?" said Father Dolan.

A small group congregated around the aqua-blue stall. "What is going on?" somebody asked.

"Two boys have locked themselves in there and won't come out."

Somebody knocked, as if the notion of knocking hadn't ever been thought of before. "Hey!" that person added, and rattled the handle, which held fast.

"Sounds to me like it's empty."

Tristan said, "We saw them go in. They had roller blades on." They called me Fatso, he thought to himself, the little twirps.

"I'm gonna die," Refugio said.

Father Dolan said, "Go find some place else to pee, Refugio. Go behind those drainpipes."

"But I'll have to lift up my skirt," Refugio said.

"I do it all the time," said Father Dolan.

Refugio ran off.

"What if they're sick?" somebody suggested. This suddenly seemed feasible. What if these boys had overdosed on something or passed out? It was completely possible.

Or what if they were in a compromising position and were afraid to come out?

"Get some help," Father Dolan said. One of the two boys in the plane tree jumped down and ran off.

"What's going on?" asked somebody who had just walked up. "Two boys are stuck in there."

"Two boys won't come out of there," somebody corrected.

The two firemen came rushing up. Finally, they had some work to do. The firecracker Judas, a pyromaniac's dream, had gone off without any trouble. This was probably the first problem the hunky firemen had had to deal with.

Tristan was staring at the widow's peak. He had an opportunity now to watch the men's bodies in motion, which he preferred to bodies at rest, posing. He was never attracted to models or magazines full of pornography; he preferred his porn on video, and often went down to the soccer field near his home just to watch men run back and forth. The firemen had what a friend called "prison body," the muscles cranked up by weightlifting and isometrics, but never allowed to stretch out with long runs or aerobic elongations.

The firemen knocked on the outhouse door, too. "This is the fire department; come on out of there." There was a pause, and then the other one said, "Or we'll have to use force."

What could they be doing in there? Tristan decided they were not playing a joke, but that they had really hurt themselves, or passed out. He looked over into the plaza and the stringy old Deer Dancer was snuffling at the big pile of flower petals and leaves that the Chapayekas had held Maria over. The drummers were getting quiet and the Deer Dancer was on his hands and knees. He pushed some of the petals around with the stuffed deer's head's antlers. What was this movement, so particular? Was that the enchanted land they were always going on about? A big pile of flowers?

Maybe. In the desert, a big pile of flowers probably looked heavenly. A tree tall enough to crucify a man probably looked motherly.

"Boys, we're breaking open the door." One of the firemen pulled something off his belt, a dumbed-down version of the Jaws of Life. He wedged it between the door and wall, and began to twist. What were they going to find on the other side? Would those boys be dead? Rushed to the hospital? Arrested for drug possession?

The door bent; it was made of plastic. It bent, and then broke, so the tool had to be used a second time. Several people coached the fireman: put it closer to the latch, don't twist so fast, use another web on the lower part. The firemen remained friendly and hunky.

One of those surges visited him again: Tristan had suddenly begun to hate the handsome fireman. Now and then, Tristan felt a hatred limned by irrational thoughts, the same kind that made him think Maria's Pentecostal activities were vulgar. But it was a real hatred. He would see this perfect person, appreciate his handsomeness, watch him work capably, communicate with others with charisma. If only handsome men would have paid attention when Tristan fell for them, if only they'd just be sensible and accept Tristan's adoration, then none of this, not the death, not the loss, nor the lapse into indulgence and promiscuity, would have been necessary. But now, every wrong in the world was this stupid handsome fireman's fault.

Nevertheless, he capably pried the door off the Porta Potti.

Inside, it was completely empty. Somehow, the boys had slipped out when everybody's back was turned, and made sure they latched it from inside. But how could they? It was like one of those Las Vegas sleight-of-hand cabinets in which a whole rhinoceros disappeared into thin air.

For the rest of the day, if anybody needed to use the toilet, they had to find a way to hold the door shut with a hand, since the latch had been snapped off.

Four girls came by, their hair let down and adorned with paper flowers. They wore white shoes. There were girls with white shoes everywhere, constantly dusting them off by rubbing the tops of the shoes on the backs of their legs, the way businessmen did with patent leathers. Didn't they know it wasn't Memorial Day yet? Tristan tried to divine the fashions that popped out of poverty. More was more: more hair, more flesh, more children. Golden-looking things. Flowers. The new Russian teacher at City College's language department could not understand the perpetual plenty of San Francisco: "Look at the melons! We must buy ten," he would say, or "Have you seen *Police Academy Four?*" and with a thump of the fist to his sternum on the "I": "I have seen *Police Academy Four.*" What was worse, the trial of deprivation or the trial of glut?

The maypole dance was beginning. He could see Refugio as part of a Matachini circle around the pole, the majority of whom were grown men. For each one, Tristan thought, there was a *manda,* a promise, a suffering that brought them to this commitment. He wondered whether there was anything he'd be willing to commit to for life. He'd had something, but it died, and sometimes the grief over it seemed the kind that kindergartners have when the class guinea pig dies. Joe had now been dead for as long as they'd been together.

Father Dolan slipped up beside him while Tristan watched the intricate choreography of the maypole dance, the ups and downs and ribbony gallantry. "Have you come here to confess, Tristan? Because I'll listen to confession."

Tristan turned to him. There'd been times when he'd had sly thoughts of going to a foreign country and confessing to a priest in Ecuador, or Slovenia, someplace where the priest would never understand the terrible things he'd say, but would absolve him anyway. Wouldn't they have to? A confession is a confession. But then he thought, I don't have to go so far. Just leaving homo San Francisco had brought Tristan to a man who wouldn't understand why the things he confessed really were sins.

What would he say? "Forgive me, Father, for I have sinned. My last confession was sixteen years ago. These are my sins: I can't grieve as well as his mother. As much as I would like to believe it, my last words to him were not 'I love you.' I have been thinking that the average life span of a human being is way too long."

Tristan looked up at the maypole. At the very top was another crown of sorts, adorned, it seemed, with little colored paper parasols on toothpicks, the kind that garnished big fluffy Polynesian drinks at the Tonga Room. On top of that, a wooden statue of a dove. Round and round the Matachini went, braiding their separate colored strands into a complicated, seemingly inextricable mess of crossings. But the dancers would undo it as well, eventually. Why couldn't Tristan? Every Matachini, Refugio included, could do the moves with confidence. They even shook gourds in their right hands, which seemed like swaggering to Tristan, showing off their ability to rub their bellies and pat their heads at the same time.

Tristan was from Michigan, the land of Gerald Ford. Tristan had trouble walking and chewing gum at the same time. He said, finally, "Ultimately, there's nothing worth saying out loud, is there, Father? I've been thinking of a hundred shocking things to make you jump out of your skin. But it sounds to me like you know them all. You've changed since the last time I've seen you."

Father Dolan smiled. "I've become earthy."

Tristan told him he wanted to wander around. It was all-out fiesta now, with firecrackers and stew and fry bread and glow wands, little kids napping on the floor of the church and Pascola dancers picking on little old godmothers and always, the grizzled, sturdy Deer Dancer, reminding Tristan, or maybe consoling him, that there was still something to do in old age, if he made it there. He was an antidote to Earl's father, a man who had made the world safe for himself for a single reason: to grow frail in it.

He tried to talk to Refugio, but the boy was busy with his friends. They were running around drinking Cokes and eating bean burros and re-collecting confetti that was everywhere, and re-throwing it. Tristan never saw the roller-blading bad boys again. They were probably on to other parties, or up on Tumamoc Hill, spray-painting their inscrutable tags on rocks rather than buildings. Signatures announcing nothing. Which painter was it who signed his name on a stack of blank paper to be sold as his work?

It was very late when he returned to the Christmas bed-and-breakfast. Among his nighttime adventures, he'd driven all over the place and gotten lost. Then, when he needed to fill the gas tank, there were no pumps open, because it was Easter.

A single moon-dished light shone over his jail-cell door. The comet had set for the night, but somewhere in the distance, searchlights decked the heavens. Maybe a new club had opened. It was Saturday night.

Opening the front door, he was surprised to watch two geckos scuttle for cover. He thought they were cute, pasty white with puppet mouths, looking for insects. Tristan turned on the porch light to draw bugs. Today would be a lizard feast. If nature would not nurture him, he would kill some of it with his own kindness.

He heard Murphy jingle through the garden to his unit. Mosquito hawks and lap dogs, Tristan thought, are drawn to the light. "Hello, my friend," he said to the Murphster. He'd never even heard Joe do his 7-Eleven voice asking for money for the princess of the town, but he was imitating it anyway. Such power, even beyond the grave.

17

Dear Joe,

WUH-woowoowoo, WUH-woowoowoo, WUH-woowoowoo! I'm surrounded by savages. Can you help me, St. Joe? I've been out in the sun too long and I think it's affecting my vision. And why in the hell, St. Joe, did you give your mother a big insurance settlement and not offer any to me? Who is the one who found you dead under the cuckoo clock?

It's been four years since you left, and what has changed? These letters don't show much. I'm a seventh grader writing your name over and over on my notebook: Tristan loves Joe, Tristan loves Joe, so many millions of times it becomes meaningless.

I'm more honest. Whenever I talk to people about you, when they want to know about your being sick, I always say it was terrific suffering. I tell them about the long drawn out part of it, and they aren't so moved, or troubled, as when I tell them about the pain, or the look of the pain, which gets them on an easier, visceral level. You know, it was horrible to see those huge catheters going into your skin, the humiliation of student doctors coming in to see you as the extraordinary case you were, looking at some open sore or other, bloody syringes, that terrible gurgle in your lungs when you breathed in deep, red call lights, swollen testicles, leg swollen solid and ready to be amputated if you were going to live long enough for it to make any difference, the way medicines went into you through tubes. Jesus, Joe, I'm still not used to it. I still see operations on PBS, the blade that cuts flesh, the place where the tube penetrates the skin, and I can never abide it. I can't imagine healing; that's my problem. I see my finger is broken, and I'd rather just let the thing get amputated than wait for it to heal.

It's Easter, time for the Resurrection. The Yaquis believe that Jesus is born again as a baby after the Crucifixion. It's like Christmas and Easter all rolled into one.

I finally had a conversation with that priest of yours. I call him *your* priest. He's yours, the way my wardrobe is today, the clothes I wear, which I never wore when you and I were alive. When you were around, it was *our* wardrobe. Don't try to get out of the blame; it's true.

Father Dolan. I told everybody I was keen on going to the big maypole dance, but the truth is, I decided to go and torture him. Why? Because I always thought he made a big deal pretending not to be gay, when he was gay—and therefore making it a big deal that he was gay. Gay is *not* a big deal. That's something both us prodigals and those prudes need to understand.

I didn't tell him anything I wanted to, I misjudged him. The whole thing is one big "I should have said." *L'esprit de l'escalier.*

To start a conversation I would have said, "I want to tell you something dangerous, Father. I feel I need to do it with you."

"Why me? Why not your own priest?" That's what he should have said. I would see he was terrified, or tired, but not both. Which?

"But you're a stranger. And you stand for the Church, and here you are doing something slightly undogmatic, wouldn't you say, and you know what else?" And just writing this down for you, Joe, I can feel my lips narrowing along with my mind and eyes, pinching to a needle-sharp point in order to poke that man. I thought him a man born to be persecuted. "I want you to suffer, Father, for Christ's sake. I want you to hear what I say and I want it to bother you!"

Not terror, but tiredness, and probably that was why Father Dolan would have stayed to hear me. What would I say? Just a list of things, like crimes, or groceries. I'd say:

We live in a world of warning signs. So many that you have to choose to ignore some of them if you're going to get anything done. Fall in love, get to Spain, make a movie. And anything I ever got, I got from ignoring the warning signs. I'd say:

I was enchanted by you, Joe. Who could see beyond your magic? Who wanted to? And when you disappeared into thin air, I was left in the dark. Maybe that is why many people begin to hate God. They don't want Jesus to be a God who was here, performed great miracles, and then vanished with a promissory note, while we remained like dogs in the mud. I'd say:

And what's left to do when beauty's greatest show on earth strikes the tent and moves out of town? When there's no unity left to beauty? You go out and grab all its pieces, all the shards of the broken, once-perfect vessel.

With God, with the magician, imagination was never necessary. Remember the bullfights, Joe? It's a ritual, but without imagination. Each time, they have to start from scratch, kill six more bulls, over and over. The crowd has to *see* the bloodshed; they aren't capable of merely imagining it. The matador is the magician. Or maybe it's the bull.

I used to marvel at the gruesome human sacrifices made by the Aztecs. Thousands of hearts pulled out of the chests by priests trained to do the work. I was bedazzled by the pure dumb brutal attempt to get at something. Something that was impossible to get at in this manner. The ritual's very nature was a firewall against the achievement of its goal.

At least Catholics have that rite, the right, you have to give them that. They have a symbolic sacrifice; memory is evoked, imagination.

Oh, I didn't want to remember your perfection, Joe. I didn't want to think. And seeking all those pieces of beauty, I mistook pleasure for loveliness.

Sex, yes, that. But all of it, opera, big rich meals, roller coasters, foreign travel, bullfights, yes, even books I used. What else was there to grab for if oblivion is the ultimate goal?

Sex, though, there's the thing. If the puritans only knew how much. How much do you think, Joe? How much have I had since you took off? Take that number and multiply it by five. Cube it. Do something mathematical to it. Make it shock you. Total strangers.

That may be the reason I've enjoyed being down here this weekend. Meeting total strangers and being close to them for a little time. If I could spend my whole life being a perfect stranger, doing everything as though it were the last time I'd be doing it, I'd be happier. But I know I can't live like that anymore.

There's that old Jerry Lewis movie, *Hook, Line, and Sinker,* where he plays a traveling salesman who learns he's dying and goes on a spending spree around the world, only to discover that his doctors have made a terrible mistake. He isn't dying at all. Then Jerry has to go underground to hide from all the people to whom he owes money.

Could it be that life imitates Jerry Lewis movies? I've maxed out my credit card (which I wouldn't have had to do if *some*body had left *me* an insurance policy), Joe, to honor that old chestnut: Your credit card balance should rise in direct correlation to the drop in your T-cell count.

I've never been good at planning ahead, with or without HIV. God, Joe, maybe that's why I fell so deeply in love with you—you were hand-to-mouth. I've got no real estate, Joe, no savings, no 401-K. I'm going to live longer, Joe. I'm expected to be a regular Schmoe, Joe. But if I'm going to be a regular Schmoe, I have some catching up to do—right now, Joe, I'm sub-Schmoe.

Do you remember when they broadcast Wagner's *Parsifal* on PBS and I made you watch with me? You're gonna love this; it's a miracle play, I told you. It was six hours long. You fell asleep and you'd wake up every hour and I'd be sitting there and you'd be incredulous and say, "Is this still on?" Now I know how you felt. I'm in this huge opera, or some huge miracle play—a Yaqui Easter Ceremony?—and even though I know it's a long dragged-out affair, I know it will end eventually. But then I wake up, and find out *this is still on.*

At La Gloria, Mik was trying to insist that I had a new boyfriend, because Earl told him I did, which is sort of my mistake. He kept coming back to it. I told him Earl was just a dumb bigmouth. "Earl thinks he can be a sensitive guy, but he's too far gone. He's permanently macho. How do you become permanently macho?"

Mik said, "When I was a boy my father used to take me outside and throw a ball at me as hard as he could." He complained bit-

terly, like I was going to get into some men-and-masculinity conversation with him.

Thank God the Deer Dancer interrupted us. He's an old, stringy,
stony thin man with rattles around his waist and leggings, shirt-
less, a white cloth binding his head and a small deer's head, its antlers woven with red cloth, strapped on with leather thongs. He
danced around like a skittish buck, on his knees at one point in a
pile of petals and leaves, pushing it all around.

I want to lord it over you, that you never grew old. But you did
grow old—I saw you shrivel up and hunch over—you used a cane
with more panache and got cranky and crotchety. Only I got to see
that. That is something even your mother can't have.

You wouldn't believe what she's done to make up for it, though.
That grave. God. They'll be pinning requests for help there soon,
boy—watch out. *Ayúdame, ayúdame!*

We went there the first night I came to town, and I was hoping to
experience some sad moment there. Whenever I try to plan my
grief, it never works out. I had to suck it in. So I thought, after the
big maypole dance, after a beer or five, I'd try again, on my own.

I tried to remember the way Mik had driven me to the cemetery
on Thursday night. I had a map but I hadn't really looked at it the
whole time. I didn't need to; everybody was taking such good care
of me. It turned out that the cemetery isn't far from Old Pascua
Village, and I must have driven all the way around the Tucson city
limits before figuring that out.

Once I got through the cemetery gates, it got even worse. No
halogen lights, no street names or directional markers, I wasn't
even sure which quadrant had your grave. The more I didn't know,
the more I had to find you. I thought that once my headlights
caught your mother's little greenhouse, I'd recognize it immediately. But, well, I hate to tell you this, Joe, but there are many ob-
sessive mothers out there in the world, and so many overdone
graves. I didn't have a flashlight, either, so I'd have to stop the car,
get out, walk to the headstone, and try to read it by the light of the
car.

They must make cemeteries like mazes on purpose. If I'd been a
great navigator I could have used the stars to find my way. Mik

says that he never gets lost no matter where he is because he sees the world as a map that's eternally shifting as he shifts. Maybe he's the ideal human. Self-sufficient even down to his own innards, a heart that shifts as he shifts like a floating directional compass needle.

But me? I'm lost. And don't try flailing your hands, over here, over here, because my goal is different now. I'm looking for your cemetery plot, not for you.

I tried. It must have been half an hour of lefts and rights and I thought I was finally coming to your stone, your little garden of Eden, your oasis. But all experience is an arch wherethrough Gleams that untraveled world whose margin fades Forever and forever when I move.

And the boys came. I don't know why I would have thought it was the same Yaqui rollerblader kids who called me the Big Belly, but I did. Faceless marauders need faces, to make them less frightening, more familiar. Bad boys are, after all, the same all over. It's just the terrain that changes; geography gives bad boys something different to do. There are stones to throw in Palestine, buses to blow up in Basque cities.

In Michigan, they blew up mailboxes with cherry bombs. For a month of my life, our mailbox was blown up nearly every day. Before breakfast, my dad would go down to the end of our driveway to clear up the usual wreckage; just another of his chores, like taking out the garbage, shoveling the sidewalk. If he only knew that it was my responsibility, for I was a typing sissy and that is what earned me countless red cherry bomb badges of courage.

Snowballs with rocks in them—oh, if Yaqui boys knew the power of those, or pine cones before they mature and split open into harmless Wiffle balls: solid green stinging missiles.

In San Francisco, the hills are perfect for illegal soapbox cars and skateboarders to go careening through the parks, terrorizing pedestrians.

And what do bad boys go for? Whatever's valuable and sacred. You've got to love them for that. The grass in graveyards in the desert. Wandering lost in your mother's shiny gold car (she's going to know I went a long way when she reads the odometer), I

came across these bad boys doing doughnuts in the good manicured grass. Ripping it up. Big divots of the stuff. Flying hunks of
sod everywhere.

On the car radio, since I changed it from your mother's easy listening, I listened to news of another rash of terrorist bombings in
the Middle East. Fanatics with bombs strapped to their bodies
were running into stores full of people and exploding themselves.
It struck me that the charge of righteousness that fueled a suicide
bomber must be something more than mere politics, or religion, or
even a show of technical and tactical know-how. There must be
something in the act that is essentially aesthetic.

I've been feeling so rebellious these past few days. I could see
myself in their shoes, running at the shopping center, dynamite
taped to my body, after four other friends had done something
similar. There! It was easy for me to imagine it—there was a
sound, a note, even a chord, a glorious one, a sense of my own
time, my own reality, the folly of terrorism is kin to the folly of
love.

I can't lie to you, Joe, the news of terrorism thrilled me. Didn't I
come down here to Arizona to desecrate? You're in the land of the
sacred and the endless ceremony, and I can't stand it anymore. Everything I can do to ruin this perfect place, I'll do. And there it is: I
have discovered the real reason for my pilgrimage to your grave.
I've come as a terrorist, to punch a hole in time and make my escape from this enchantment.

I got out of the car, turned off the headlights, and watched the
boys destroying. Their headlights would hit tombstones and I'd
see the dates on them. It was like flashcards—I'd do the ages:
1931 to 1969 equals 38. Older than me. 1972 to 1987 equals 15.
Younger than me. 1947 to 1981 equals 34. My age on the dot.

I was sure they must have seen me. Or at least the car. But
maybe they thought I was a couple making out, or a plainclothes
policeman. Anyway, they weren't tough enough for my taste, ultimately. They never knocked down a headstone, and they never got
gutsy enough to come over and investigate me or your mother's
car. After a while, they'd done all the peeling out they could possibly do, and they drove off. They left me.

I saw a well-tended grave. Don't worry; it wasn't yours. I would have recognized the brittle bush a mile away. I turned my head-lights back on so I could see, and the name on the headstone said "Goldfarb," and just one date, 1996. Does that mean it was a Jew-ish baby? There wasn't a Star of David, but there wasn't a cross, either. There were tons of flowers, though. I just started tossing them every which way.

Then I got in the car and left. I had intended to leave something on your grave, a memento, my picture of Jesús Malverde, but I couldn't find your stone, so I kept it. It means a lot more to me than it does to you, anyway. Do you want to know where I got it? I came for Jesús, not just for you. Magicians have such huge egos, don't they, to think I only came to see about you.

I want to tell you about something that happened on that disastrous trip to Nogales we took with Mik way back. Do you remember? How the bullfights made you sick? How I had my eyebrows shaved off? I've never told you about something else that happened there, in that time I was out wandering the city on my own before we met in the afternoon at the bull ring. It has to do with sick. Do I feel guilty about that? You were getting sick then, you know, and not up to getting naked with me.

 18

To start with, Tristan thought, it's only funny to an American that his name was Jesús, the jerk, except that it wasn't that funny in English, either. His mouth tasted like cigarettes—what a surprise. In Mexico, of all places.

Jesús sat in the Café Figueroa at the table next to Tristan's, drinking the local beer. He wasn't even that handsome. He was thin. Gap-toothed. *Hard-bitten*, Tristan thought to himself, that's what that term means. But he had this hair, this chocolate sheen so many Mexican boys have that made Tristan think of satin-smooth whipped cake frosting. And he was interested in Tristan. He'd ordered his beer at the bar and spotted Tristan and smiled, showing that curious gap between his teeth, and that's flattering in any country. Tristan was susceptible to it.

Tristan liked Nogales so far. He'd got a haircut and a margarita and had a nice chat with the barber and the bartender. And so he'd become too confident. He began to Understand Spanish. A few great successes, in fact, like negotiating a haircut—had made him triumphant and sloppy. So that this—this!—to go to a café and sit down with a beer and meet this boy, this Jesús, and converse with him in Spanish, why, of course he had the ego of a conquistador.

Jesús sat down but stayed silent at first. Of course he knew Tristan was a tourist. His hair was not chocolate brown. He had a map.

Everybody was smoking: that harsh black tobacco, which can cloud up a bar so that you need to crawl on the floor to get at the remaining oxygen. The café was blue from the stuff. It was a lively afternoon. Incongruously, a baby began to cry from some back corner, perhaps upstairs by the pool table.

A baby in a gay bar? He enjoyed the silliness, the naughtiness, the shocking inappropriateness of hearing an infant ten feet from men groping each other's crotches, slipping the occasional tongue.

And Tristan had one of those moments. It was a moment of pure joy, a Wordsworth surprise that makes you feel sheepish. But joy it is, a thing Tristan collected and collated, tried to pick apart so that he might know the cause of pleasure, its recipe. In this case, he approximated: his meeting Joe's mother was a success, he had impressed the friends, he had seen the prickly Southwest, he'd got a haircut for four bucks, the margarita and beers were taking effect, a moderately cute boy had taken an interest in him, he had exactly ten pesos left, which was enough to pay for his drinks and get a cab to the bullfight ring, where he was to rendezvous with Joe and Mik, and now—a baby was crying in a gay bar!

These moments of pure joy also made him weak, unreliable, giddy. Joy is a misunderstanding of the true situation of the world. Joy is like thinking you know a foreign language just because you can communicate in it.

Tristan said, in that joy, in Spanish, to the gap-toothed Jesús, "That baby is crying because everybody is smoking in here."

Jesús said, "That baby is crying," and he slid his beer glass onto Tristan's table and slid down the bench, "because he doesn't have any cigarettes."

Tristan asked the waiter for two more beers. Jesús introduced himself. He was from Ciudad Juárez, an industrial town where Tristan had spent two hours waiting for a bus connection on a previous trip, a few years ago.

Jesús was also polite and asked Tristan where he'd traveled. For a variety of reasons, Tristan did not tell Jesús about Joe.

Jesús put his hand on Tristan's crotch under the table. Tristan returned the gesture. Jesús was wearing loose chinos and no underwear, Tristan thought. As he groped, Tristan stared into space like a child peeing in a swimming pool.

"Do you have a place to go?" he asked, charmingly direct.

"Unfortunately, I don't," Tristan said, thinking of Joe tapping his foot outside the bull ring.

"I know a place," Jesús said. "They charge for an hour and it is discreet." He described a house run by a man who offered privacy to anyone for a few pesos.

The waiter arrived with their beers. He didn't smirk, but Tristan knew he knew what was going on.

Jesús was asking him a question. Tristan didn't quite get the exact meaning of it but it went something like, "You do realize what we're doing here, don't you? I mean, you're a man and I'm a man, and we're going to need a place because what we want to do together isn't appropriate for my own home or your *residencia*." Of course Tristan understood his point, the need to ask such a question.

"Yes, I understand," Tristan replied. What two men might do together could run the gamut of mischief: vandalism, a drug deal, a bank heist.

In broken English, Jesús said, endearing as a baby animal, "So you like mens?" He unzipped Tristan under the table, and Tristan made himself believe that nobody could possibly see this through all the smoke.

"*Sí, sí*," Tristan said. It was flattering to think Jesús might think he was straight.

Jesús began to ask vague questions requiring a yes or no answer about what Tristan liked about him and what he liked about mens in general. It was all filler, this part of talking, and isn't it funny how language is downplayed in the way science fiction movies downplay it—there is hardly ever a problem with communication. We meet Desiree, the queen of the moon women, and she speaks English with a slight Hungarian accent. The astronaut flies a thousand years into his own future to find apes who've learned to speak perfect Queen's English.

"Let's go." Jesús pulled at him.

Outside, the streets were busy with the afternoon crowds. Everybody in Nogales loves a party, and how could Tristan feel unsafe or even sleazy with so many women and men and occasional crying babies doing the same thing? It is impossible to feel guilty in Spanish; the language won't allow it. You cannot say: "You have to do it." You say, "It must be done."

Jesús walked in front of him. Look how his hair grows naturally to a point at the nape of his neck, like the curl on a kewpie doll. When Tristan traveled he wished to be alone and yet surrounded, to be simultaneously unselfed and selfish.

He was right: the house wasn't far. The building was on a little off-street. It was stately, probably the home of a fine family many years ago. Jesús rang the bell. He knew what he was doing.

The door was opened by a short cheerful bald man, the kind of guy who scalped bullfight tickets. Under his left arm he carried a roll of paper towels. He ushered them both in. They stood in a wide foyer with an immense staircase ahead. Two men came down the stairs, and Jesús knew one of them. They clapped each other on the shoulder. What fun! This was beyond sex, this was *National Geographic.*

"This way," said the little proprietor. He had a low center of gravity, and would place well at a tractor pull in an American county fair. He led them up the staircase past many rooms, some with doors open, showing girls and boys, boys and boys, girls and girls. In one room a girl sat on a boy's lap and a homey fire was burning here in hot midday May. Couples would glance out at them as they passed by, and Tristan felt some weird camaraderie, which perhaps he had no right to. On the landing of every flight of stairs rested a spittoon. Flocked wallpaper. Shabby elegance. Their charming host pushed open a door and used his free arm to present the room like a prize.

What he did next stuck in Tristan's mind as something important, a ritual whose significance Tristan never quite understood. He took the roll of paper towels, carefully pulled off eight precise squares, and rested them on a dinged-up credenza. One, two, three, four, five, six, seven, eight.

He smiled again and left them. The room was well-kept. A big bed, three comfortable chairs, flowery old rugs over glorious parquet floors, linoleum wall decor up to the wainscoting, all dusted and swept. The bedspread was cream-colored with little roses. It had several stains, but Tristan decided that they were clean stains.

Jesús shucked off his clothes. Around his dark neck he had one of those gold chains, garish no matter how simple they are. As he leaned over to untie his shoes the chain pulled tight and perfectly flat against the tendons in his neck and Tristan wanted to run his finger along there, maybe slip his finger beneath and feel its tightness.

That's where his hands most liked to be, between a rock and a hard place. He liked the spandex on good mittens that gripped his wrists. He liked fingerpaints. He liked to reach into a man's pants with the belt still fastened and go even farther, wriggling down through the elastic band of underwear. It gave him great pleasure to think that Santa Claus sometimes got stuck in chimneys and that one might slip a finger into the kitchen faucet and get it caught there.

Tristan wanted to put his finger between the necklace and the neck, and so he did. Jesús looked up with pooling dark eyes. He tripped Tristan onto the bed and pulled his shirt over his head and proceeded to wet down Tristan's body with his tongue, as if Tristan needed a new coat of varnish.

Everything is different when you are a traveler—except sex, which is gloriously the same, boring, regular, a limitation of intentions, singular, just one kind of desire as opposed to all the millions that confuse the world. Sex was focus for Tristan. It was prayer. And so he achieved that other goal of the traveler: to be familiar in a foreign place and to find home out in the bush. Others find it at the foreign newsstand with its rack of Sidney Sheldon novels or at a McDonald's.

Jesús was Tristan's hot dog, his T-shirt, his "wow." Jesús had technique, he knew what mens like, he used his hands in conjunction with his mouth, and he stood up at times and let Tristan objectify him. He had nice legs and his calf muscles were in the shape of two skinned chicken breasts. A dribble of hair from his navel splayed to his sternum like a retreating glacial moraine. It was nice to look at. At times, when he hunkered forward on all fours, the gold chain hung low and slipped over his chin, a little trap. He wouldn't take it off. Tristan liked that. It made Tristan feel superior. It made him feel hard.

Everything is different when you're traveling except sex, but you notice sex more. You do things during sex that you wouldn't do at home, as you wouldn't look up at skyscrapers in your own downtown.

Tristan lay back and let Jesús enter him. *"¿Tienes un condón?"* Jesús asked, at least. No, there weren't any, but Tristan let him get inside anyway. How to explain? Wasn't there any place on earth free of the danger? If anywhere, then here.

With his head hanging upside down over the side of the bed he could just see the corners of the paper towels (eight of them; could he see all eight?) curling up. Perhaps that's why the ritual was so important to him, the tearing of each square: when Tristan concentrated on the orgasm, he was looking at the towels.

The sex didn't take a long time. Boredom can't be sustained. Jesús was pleased with what he had wrought, a task accomplished, and he hopped off the high bed and grabbed all the paper towels in one careless handful and wasted them by clumsily daubing at Tristan's wet belly and chest as if he were cleaning up any spill.

Tristan took his cue as Jesús started to dress—perhaps Tristan's time was up, and the short bald man would return soon and ask for more rent on the space.

And, as Tristan sat lacing up his complicated hiking shoes, Jesús said: *"Mi dinero."*

"What?" Tristan asked, incredulous.

This is no lie; he was incredulous. Tristan worked very hard at not becoming too jaded—he prided himself on being shocked. Shocked by airlines that still put Bible verses on the tray with his meal, shocked by travel guides that did not include his favorite landmarks, shocked by pickpockets at busy terminals, by lodges that thought "family style" is a way people could possibly enjoy eating a meal.

"No tengo," Tristan said flatly and furiously. It was Jesús' turn to be incredulous. But Tristan was telling the truth: he had spent his money on the beers. Jesús pressed Tristan, and suddenly Tristan was an idiot with the language. Jesús had two words that he could say, and Tristan had two words that he could say.

The insult! That Tristan would need to pay for it like an ugly or married man! Jesús should pay *him*. He was so mediocre, so much less remarkable than, for God's sake, so many free sexual experiences Tristan had . . . experienced.

Tristan stood up, the shoelaces tied, and tromped out of the room. He didn't even dispose of the soiled paper towels. He passed the spittoons on each landing and never looked back through those wide doors. He no longer identified any secret comrades in any of the rooms. Jesús was like a dog that hadn't been walked just behind him, chanting those same two stupid words. Tristan felt foul and disappointed. The night was hot and the streets were crowded and there were broken bottles on ugly, ordinary, gray flagstones. The air in tires in Mexico is kept low to navigate the uneven cobbling. They let off a squealing noise that terrorized Tristan as cars approached down narrow streets, because there was no sidewalk to jump on. How could a moment of pure joy come out of this?

But Jesús never scared him. He was too small; Tristan could take him. As Tristan walked he decided that he could pretend not to understand Jesús, he could walk and walk all evening and never return to the hostel until Jesús gave up. Surely he had other tricks to catch?

They passed by the café, which Tristan could see through the windows was now too crowded for anyone to sit down. When the doors opened the building belched a cloud of smoke.

Jesús wouldn't quit. Tristan turned down another street, and he was never alone. There was never an opportunity for Jesús to extort or be violent. There was traffic and market in every road, ordinary, safe people.

"No tengo," Tristan said for the hundredth time. He passed by the barbershop, and he remembered that this was the turn he had taken to go toward the café. Tristan decided that it would contribute to Jesús' despair if he were to turn that way again and walk in circles, to prove he had no intention of leaving until Jesús left. Tristan thought about the ordinary sex. He thought about his ridiculous idea of wanting to be alone and yet surrounded at the same time—all Tristan really wanted was to be alone. In his mind he tried out the idea of paying Jesús and then made himself angry with that fantasy.

It was a challenge not to look at him. Tristan concentrated on the boring flagstones. When he circled back and came in sight of what he now realized was the brothel, he hoped to see Jesús throw his hands in the air and peel off, cut his losses, head for the café, and find another fool.

But among the crowd of chatting and loitering people, Jesús was back on familiar turf. Tristan turned back and watched Jesús motion toward friends hidden in the crowd, party imposters who were boys like him. One, two, three, four prostitutes slipped out of the crowd and congealed into a gang in league with Jesús. It was like watching spies unmask themselves.

He broke into a run. He ran and ran. Tristan remembered the paper towels, the gray flagstones, and his lungs burned as he ran down that boulevard full of traffic and people shouting out of their cars things in Spanish he couldn't understand.

He ran at full tilt for fifteen minutes, the fastest and longest he'd ever run. Air scraped his throat like he'd swallowed sand, and, of all those boys chasing behind him, it was Jesús who was fastest. He kept just behind Tristan and tried now and then to trip him up.

There was a taxicab at a stoplight near a confusing roundabout. The light was changing, and Tristan leapt into the back seat of the cab and locked the door. He waited for the driver to step on the gas. But the driver stayed, and Tristan watched as Jesús and one, two, three, four friends caught up and regrouped. They stared at him through the window.

"Go!" Tristan screamed at the driver.

The driver turned off the ignition and blocked traffic. He got out of the car and stood next to Jesús and his gang. "Get out," he said to Tristan. Everybody had their two words, the ones they could get by on.

Outside, he saw Jesús' face, the only familiar one among that gaggle of boys and the cowardly lazy cabbie. Foreign yet familiar was Jesús right then.

Tristan got out of the cab. The driver drove off: he was the greatest enemy, pure evil; Jesús was merely fate and the end that must be faced.

"How much?" Tristan said to them.

"Twenty pesos."

The amount was ridiculously low, about twenty bucks. Tristan could have squandered that much on souvenirs. *"No tengo,"* he tried again but didn't even believe it himself this time. "Where is the bank?" he asked. He slipped and used the word for savings and loan, instead of bank.

Why would you want a savings and loan? they wanted to know; banks are closed. "Credit card," Tristan said.

Miracles are always ordinary and local. Lazarus rises from the dead. There's enough bread and wine to go around. Strange, foreign miracles may happen, but they're unrecognizable and go unreported. If a refrigerator fell from heaven and crushed Elijah, he wouldn't have reported it in the Bible because he could not have conceived of the object. If God revealed to Moses a new color in the spectrum, Moses didn't have a name for it, and it has faded into history, undescribed. But a bank within eyeshot of the site of his own death—that was a local, not foreign, miracle.

Less than a block away from where the cabdriver had turned off his engine, there was a bank whose facade was being redone, surrounded by scaffolding, its cash machine still operating, set into the old gray stone, more boring real flagstone with a miracle glowing green in that dangerous place.

They escorted and gathered close around Tristan to make sure he wouldn't run again. Tristan pulled his credit card out. Would they hit him, take it, and run now? Would they wait until he punched in his personal identification number, then push him aside, and select the highest amount of cash? Or would they wait until he extracted the cash and go for the card and the cash both? When, oh when, would they kill Tristan and put him out of his misery?

The card was in. He pressed the little picture of the American flag so he could understand, in the English language, the selections on the screen. He clung to the English the way people in a museum full of abstract art run to the realistic sculpture of a human figure. He looked at his own signature on the back of his card, which looked like a foreign language too.

And then Tristan did something strange: with his right hand he made the sign of the cross. One, two, three, four: Father, Son, Holy, Ghost. It was some atavistic habit from his childhood that he'd so carefully pushed down, but to do it was like breathing. He looked behind at Jesús and the boys. Were they offended by his bringing God into the picture? Apparently, they did not think anything of it. Hurry up, Tristan thought they said.

They talked among themselves, and Tristan didn't understand a thing they were saying. The English on the machine was clear: How much would you like? One hundred, fifty, or twenty pesos? The miracle of the pesos: he selected the lowest amount. Out came a crisp bill. Now they will grab it. Now they will kick him in the stomach. But they didn't grab the pesos. They waited until Tristan pulled it out, retrieved his card and the receipt slip. They waited until he put his wallet back in order. Tristan would like to say he took his time out of pride, but really he couldn't think of what to do next. Why hadn't they killed him yet?

He handed Jesús the twenty perfect pesos. Now they will kill him, now. But this was Mexico, and not America, and Jesús had got what he wanted, and they all gathered around Tristan and said, "There, you see, shake hands; give us your hand." They wanted to shake hands!

Shocked, Tristan looked at them, and, if he had had skirts to gather about him, he would have. He said in Spanish, "Mexico is very beautiful, but Nogales is a bad whore!" At least he thought he did. They wrinkled their broad pretty foreheads, all of them, and wondered what the hell he was trying to say. Jesús took a card out of his pocket—a business card?—and shoved it into Tristan's shirt pocket.

Tristan strode off, and the last of that miracle was that he was within a block of the bullfighting ring. He looked back, and the boys were already almost invisible to him, hiding under all that scaffolding, green in the glow of the cash machine.

A package tour bus full of old American ladies was unloading and filing into the bull ring. He could see Joe and Mik leaning against a little ticket gazebo, and Mik was checking his watch. The bus pulled out, then stopped, blocking his view of those two. Tristan reached into his shirt pocket.

And he saw Jesús once again. Only now he had his thin, hard-bitten face in profile and didn't look so hungry. Tristan could see bright eyes and hair the color of—yes, chocolate—and there was a halo, a definite golden globe around his head, and there was a prayer on the back of the picture. On the front it said, "Jesús Malverde, *ruega por nosotros.*" Years went by, during which he seroconverted thanks to Jesús, and during which he discovered that this was not Jesús' calling card but a gift of his patron saint, Malverde, who watched over the pimps and hustlers and other bad boys of Nogales.

19

That night, after returning from the maypole dance and the conversation with Father Dolan, he dreamed and remembered the dream vividly, as he always did when he slept in a strange bed, even one as comfortable as this. He dreamed he was being pursued, and the pursuers wore colorful dress-up clothes but were obviously dangerous and relentless. He dreamed that he was well hidden and they were walking past his hiding place, but then they came right back to him after they looked like they had already gone.

The dream only ended when he woke up at the sound of a car door being slammed. He got out of his bed and enjoyed the cold painted concrete floor of the adobe on the bottoms of his bare feet. He slapped over to the window and could see Mrs. Jimenez dressed up for Easter sunrise mass. She was wearing a powder-blue dress—the color of the bathtub grotto in Mik's yard—and matching pillbox hat and a white purse. She had an amazing corsage of orange flowers from her garden. Against the dust and gravel and iron bars on the windows of the adobe across the street, she looked like one of those new-styled television commercials in which everything was black and white except for the decidedly bold color of the product for sale. She was something he would buy, definitely, Tristan oddly thought in this drowsy state.

He was almost trying to bruise the balls of his feet the way he walked on them back across the delicious floor, and it wasn't until he was back in bed and ready to doze that he had the vague hunch that she was wearing the same dress this morning that she'd worn to Joe's funeral.

Was such a thing possible? Wouldn't she have worn a more sobering color? No, no: he saw her again lunging at the box of ashes. He'd grabbed her by the bright-blue buttoned sleeve and had the inappropriate thought that he'd worn a tuxedo in the same shade of blue on his junior prom night.

The funeral was sickeningly sweet to him, like a child's first communion. Maria had sung a song from *Beauty and the Beast* in the organ loft and Tristan felt exposed and central as he walked into a church already full.

Some "close" friend of Joe's—his prom date, somebody told him later, somebody Joe'd never mentioned in his life and who was never mentioned again—gave a farewell speech that she simultaneously delivered in sign language, and everybody cried. It was a funeral mass, so it was long and consolingly dull. Tristan spent most of the liturgy pondering a prayer card with the picture of Jesus with two fingers raised, that soft heroin-ish glaze over the eyes. Why did people always confuse passivity with otherworldliness? "Joseph I. Jimenez," it said, just like on the gravestone, and beneath that, that hastily chosen anecdote "Footprints" printed in gold. "Footprints" was the precious story of a man who dies and meets God. God shows the man his life depicted as a long walk on the beach with two sets of footprints—one set for the man, another set belonging to God; and at the point of greatest hardship, there is strangely only one set of prints. "This is evidence of abandonment," says the man. "That is where I carried you," God explains.

Pish. At some point, Tristan nearly destroyed everything by laughing uproariously there in this pall of irrational death, for he came upon the notion that Joe's meeting with God might better be entitled not "Footprints," but "Dragmarks." Oh, how he had wanted to laugh then.

Everything finished in an orderly manner. Tristan didn't have to do a thing. Maria shuttled him around. The altar society was a brood of Tucson matrons whose wardrobes all seemed built around their kitchen aprons. Everybody seemed relieved by having a job to perform. Tristan felt capable of doing nothing.

The feeling of that time was very particular and very memorable. It was the same as when he'd fallen out of a tree when he was ten and landed on his finger, breaking it backward. There had been no pain there; pain was all in the adjacent finger, which had merely jammed. He could not cry for Joe, but when clumsy Tristan dropped a plate of food on the cold adobe floor, he became a wailing, gnashing ninny.

There were tons of food at the wake. A very terrified tiny woman with big round glasses that magnified her horror of being so close to a known homosexual said, "So, you're from C-c-c-california," and he had said, "No, actually, I grew up in northern Michigan," which he realized was not the correct answer. She had only wanted a yes or no. She said, "Oh" and ran out into the garden.

The people milled about him, not really up to engaging him in conversation. Tristan's shoelaces came untied again. They went in stages, untied shoelaces. For months he'd go and tie them once in the morning and that was that. He'd kick them off without untying them in the evening (Joe said that when he was a child his mother, an immaculate housekeeper, would tie his two shoes together in tight knots if she found he'd slipped out of his shoes before untying them). Then there'd be a two-day-long spate of slippage. Since he'd arrived in Tucson for the funeral, the slippage thing had left him nearly tripping down the aisle of the church, and causing a hazard among the buffet tables. It was why he'd dropped his plate.

The first time he ever met Earl, Maria's then-controversial husband, was there in the living room with a second-try plateful of three-bean and macaroni salad. Tristan made a cheerful tisking sound and observed his own undone state, then made a face at this guy, who he'd later find out was Earl, who'd been watching.

"Hey, Boss," said this guy, "Let me show you how the b-ball pros tie 'em so they don't get loose."

Like a servant, this guy went down on one knee and did a little trick involving a second loop around the bow. Trade? Tristan thought in a naughty slip, God, at his own boyfriend's funeral. But no, this guy was a veritable glut of heterosexual signifiers, "b-ball," calling him Boss, those sporty golf slacks, that pantomime of a golf swing or a forward pass or a slam dunk. Sometimes

Tristan felt sorry for the restricted vocabulary of the straight. In a way, excusing oneself from masculinity was a huge relief.

This guy was finishing the knot when Maria came up and introduced him to Tristan as Earl, her husband. Their two sons scuttled up, at the time four and two years old, and Maria made them laugh: "What's Daddy doing?" They were laughing, but at whom? Daddy ridiculous on the floor, or Tristan ridiculously unable to tie his own shoelaces?

In those days, Maria and Mrs. Jimenez used to say under their breath that Eric (THAT was his name!), the older boy, Captain Twitch, was just like Joe—quiet, interested in books, always lining up his toy cars in rows. Tristan didn't know whether they said this with fear—oh, no, another gay one!—or as a way to hold onto something living, a replacement for Joe.

Mrs. Jimenez came up and joined in the laughter. She was nearly hysterical, swinging from despair to hilarity. She was laughing only because the children were laughing.

"Tristan, I'd like you to meet Father Dolan. Father Dolan, this is Tristan Broder. He teaches English literature. He lived with Joe. He was Joe's best friend." Tristan liked the forcefulness with which she said this. It was said not to hide their relationship, but to reveal it.

But Tristan knew just by looking at Father Dolan that such revelations were not necessary. Father Dolan was "of the church." Father Dolan was a big homo.

Mrs. Jimenez drifted away. Maria and Earl did too, long before, since Maria was divorced, and Pentecostal, and remarried. Father Dolan was thin-boned, possibly younger than Tristan.

The priest was as nervous as the little altar society lady had been. He knew that Tristan knew. "Did he suffer much?" Father Dolan asked, wincing.

Tristan looked at him. He'd told everybody, everybody, everybody that Joe had not suffered, not even a little. Painkillers worked and he went quietly in his sleep. But stabbing into macaroni, Tristan said conspiratorially, as if passing off a baton to somebody on his relay team, "Oh, yes. Horribly. You can't even imagine."

The last month had been maddening, because Joe wouldn't quit. Allergic to or intolerant of the painkilling drugs, even most kinds of morphine, he was usually curled in pain. The Kaposi's sarcoma ran rampant through him, swelled one leg so big with fluids and a purple color that it made the other shriveled leg look like a mismatch, a Barbie doll limb stuck onto a GI Joe. A chiropractor, hunky and healthy and with an atrociously symbolic name (Mort? Amour? He couldn't recall any more) came every other day, pro bono, to work on Joe's spine and leg. It was a lesson in futility, but the chiropractor was always cheerful and kind and Tristan always felt compelled to make him lunch after they'd put Joe back in bed.

"Does he make you feel any better?" Tristan kept asking after the hunk left.

Joe would shrug and in a thinning voice tell him it was nice to just have a change of scene.

Oh, that disappearing voice. Even four years later, Tristan still had a tape of Joe leaving the message, "You've reached Joe and Tristan, but we're not home, so leave us a message after the long tone." On his voice mail at school, Joe had left him a squeaky, faint voice after another of his painful chemo cocktails, "Hey, Dude, I just wanted to let you know what happened at the doctor's today, so give me a call. Bye, Honey. I love you so much," and that sound of a feeble person unable to put the phone on the hook without sliding it all over the place, and then that officious and cheerful lady who spoke for all voice mail everywhere, saying, "This message will be saved for—ten—days."

Then Joe died over the weekend, and Tristan would call over the following week into his own saved messages, just to hear Joe once more, and "This message will be saved for—five—days." Five, four, three, how could he save the message to some mailbox that would hold it indefinitely? He couldn't get ahold of the systems administrator at the college to find out, and he'd lost the printed directions to his own phone. There'd been a day of useless playing about and somehow, in all the experiments with that last sad message, Tristan hit the wrong button on his keypad and the message was erased.

Charles, the annoying, had been carting Joe back and forth to the hospital for those last days of treatment, while Tristan, who could have canceled classes, clung to the regularity of work, going in every day. He couldn't stand watching Joe hurt. He spent more time entertaining Joe's visitors than helping Joe himself.

He told all this to Father Dolan, didn't skip a thing about the pain. "He'd rally, you know, and get hungry, so I'd put some food on the stove, and just the smell of the food would fill him up, so that by the time it came to the bed, he wouldn't touch it. I had to keep lids on pots and hide food until the last minute. Then he'd just throw it back up."

The rooms of the house were filled with the coffee percolator sound of the oxygen machine, and when Joe went out, he had a portable cart with an oxygen tank. Sometimes he'd try to take the oxygen feed off his face, but that was only for a couple of friends who he wanted to think that he was doing a lot better.

"The last twenty-four hours were the worst," Tristan said. "Mostly because he suddenly seemed to be full of energy. But a friend who was visiting said he saw Joe take a handful of Marinol, the pill form of marijuana, and a doctor had successfully figured out that Joe could handle the morphine patches, fentanyl, which releases the drug through the skin. Joe woke up and sat straight up, ate a big bowl of something, watched television with what looked like concentration, and asked for two straws for his soda.

"Why two straws?" Tristan had asked.

Joe went into one of his straight-ahead stupors, and then looked up to say, "For my journey."

Tristan told this to the priest, who sat listening, as he always did, with an expression, not of pity, not of concern, but horror. What did he think, that taking the robes meant he'd be able to escape the troubles of the world? Tristan said, "You know, I never used to see any realism in those old bloody crucifixes and mosaics of the agony of Christ. I thought it was exaggeration to prove a point. Not until I actually saw Joe, who had laid in bed so long that even that was painful, was I able to believe in any real suffering on Christ's part." That was a sin to say, it was also faithless and unimaginative, but it was true.

"And isn't it sad that while Christ suffered for all of us, kind of a redemptive trust fund for all of us, Joe did all that suffering for zero dividends?" Tristan was practically escorting Father Dolan out into Mrs. Jimenez's garden. When he was with a stranger, Tristan could be bold, cruel, erotic. "For diddly? For squat? I feel like starting a religion around him; he was such a good boy, you know."

That night before Joe died, Tristan had wondered whether he should call Mrs. Jimenez and postpone her trip once again. She'd scheduled a flight on Monday, and this was Saturday. He sat next to Joe in a chair reading to him. They'd gone through a dozen books, and now they were on short stories because they were the only thing Joe could stand. "Flannery O'Connor, Father, do you know her? Very Catholic writer. I was reading 'A Good Man Is Hard to Find.' Not very sentimental, is it? He was sitting on his bed and he had one of those special mattresses that inflated in one part and then deflated while another part inflated, to prevent bedsores. He had a big bowl of alphabet soup and was actually eating it, but he kept zoning out, he'd taken so many painkillers."

Joe's eyes were glazed, and Tristan thought it was the same kind of glaze you see when a man is truly lusting after somebody. He wasn't eating the soup now but staring at it. Tristan had put the book face down in his lap and lain a hand on Joe's bony gray shoulder, and studied the skin that he'd once fallen in love with, smooth, olive, sinuous with muscle and a kind of wrestler's torque; now it was riddled with every kind of skin irritation, acne, sore. Truly, this was the plague. "What are you looking at?" Tristan asked Joe.

Joe looked up like a drunk at a bar who had passed out and been awakened by the bartender, denying the charge of drunkenness. He grinned. "I'm looking for Waldo!" Waldo. The little man lost in a crowd in the picture game books for children. Joe had turned "Where's Waldo?" into an existential question.

These were his last words to Tristan. Tristan tucked him in. Tristan rewound this memory a million times and convinced himself that his own last words to Joe were, "I love you," but that conviction might have been merely self-conciliatory. He went up to bed.

In the morning, the phone rang and it was an old high school friend calling. Tristan was groggy and tumbled down the stairs in his robe and picked up the phone before realizing Joe's bed was empty. He saw Joe slumped under the cuckoo clock, his head against the weighted leaden pine cones, the weight of which pulled the time through the clock and made the little cuckoo come out on his spring. Therefore, the clock had stopped, and told Tristan the exact time Joe had died: 5:37. But then again, that clock always did run fast.

Tristan told his friend he'd have to call him back; Joe was out of bed and had to be put back in.

"Have you ever found a dead body on your floor, Father?" Tristan asked. "You don't quite know what to do. I thought maybe he just sat there because he ran out of energy. I'd found him sleeping on the couch a couple of times because he'd gotten up to go to the bathroom and didn't have the strength to go all the way to the bed. So I thought that this was another one of those things. But when I reached to wake him he was cold, just cold like an object, like a chair you need to warm up with your own body before it gets comfortable."

When he realized that Joe was, in fact, dead, Tristan had paced the room like a mother animal of some sort whose baby had died, a mother monkey, maybe, arms over head, screeching. Did he screech? Probably.

He also did what any mother monkey would do, and picked up the body, all skin and bones, light as a bird now, purple and gray, all the wrong colors for a human being.

"And what do you think of this, Father? Now that you've performed the funeral and dedicated him to God or whatever, I just think you should know this. When I was picking up his body and hauling it back to the bed so that the coroner could look him over, and, you know, sign off, I found four fentanyl patches on his body. Four! He'd put them all over, without my noticing. Imagine the resourcefulness. I didn't think he had it in him."

"So," the priest had said, "he overdosed? On morphine?"

"Exactly," Tristan said, and suddenly told the priest that he just realized that the tuna casserole he was eating was delicious, with a corn chip crust rather than a potato chip crust.

Had he been horrible enough? Had he tortured this man enough, caused him to doubt? Caused him to think that perhaps he had given the funeral for not only a homosexual, but a suicidal homosexual?

Despite the fact that this story was meant to burn, cauterize, or purify Father Dolan, it was Tristan who ended up bawling, and it was a funny feeling to be eating food that tasted so good and crying over it, too. "Of course, I pulled three of them off before the coroner got there, because I didn't want any trouble. It was a good thing I checked."

20

He woke up again and it felt like half a day later. It was Murphy, on his chest, licking his face. Jingle, jingle, jingle went his collar.

Mrs. Jimenez was coming in with a big pot of coffee and a breakfast of a Spanish omelette and a strudel and another of her slobbery grapefruits. "Happy Easter! May I join you?" Mrs. Jimenez had brought out two sets of silverware, two plates.

"Please, oh good!" said Tristan.

She was still in the spring outfit, and now Tristan could see she'd had her hair done for Easter. The matted wig look was momentarily gone, and so were all the rednesses and roughnesses. Tristan poured coffee for both of them. "Happy Easter," he said.

"I hope this is an appropriate Easter breakfast," she said, breathlessly, situating herself at the table. She stopped to put a hand with lacquered nails the color and sheen of candy apples on his shoulder. He hadn't bothered to put on clothes, just pulled on a terry robe. "A friend gave me a cookbook that's called, I'm not kidding you, *Cooking with Christ.* I honestly tried to use it, but there's something gruesome about cherry-filled blintzes to honor the Slaughter of the Innocents!" Tristan could see that she was at the outer limits of the possibility of naughtiness, so he honored her by laughing with his mouth in a you're-in-trouble "o." Come to think of it, the cherry blintzes did seem in bad taste.

"Have you been enjoying that Yaqui thing?" she asked. "There's butter in that covered bowl."

"Very much," said Tristan. "More than Maria and Mik. More than I expected. But I'm funny that way."

"Heavens, Easter mass is a half hour longer and I think I won't be able to sit still for that. Are you going back today?"

"I don't know," said Tristan. The eggs were perfect. "I'm funny that way, too. Get to the most important day, the whole point, and I can't celebrate. He is risen? I'm not ready." Would she ever acknowledge the fact that he was far more sacrilegious than she'd ever experienced?

"*Caro,* I felt just the same after my husband died," she said. Her husband?

The strudel was sugary. He'd put sugar in his coffee, too, not a thing he usually did, but it seemed to go with his new unhealthy regimen of whiskey sours, lard, salditos, caffeine. Sugar had, lately, made him feel feverish. Was he becoming a diabetic? Was his liver on its last legs? God, he'd become too aware of what went on in his own body. It felt womanly. There was a mole on his right shin and he swore that it had changed color in the last month.

"You never talk about your husband," he said. Mr. Jimenez had died long before Tristan met Joe. He was an invisible man who wasn't often talked about. Joe never seemed to miss or resent him, nor had Maria said much. The fact that Mr. Jimenez's grave looked ordinary while there'd been an honest attempt to turn Joe's into a roadside shrine added to that. But, truth to tell, Joe had a photograph of his father when he was young, a close-up of his face in some kind of military uniform. He was a looker. Tristan had kept the photo, even displayed it. Gay friends would come over and they'd say, "Stop the presses, who's that?"

"He was fifteen years older than me," she said, "more like a father than a husband. I married him because my parents forbade me."

"This sounds like a family trait," Tristan said, stabbing at the omelette.

Mrs. Jimenez narrowed her eyes. "Mr. Jimenez was not a truck driver."

Tristan didn't mean to start a fight, so he decided to side with her for the moment. "And I'm sure he'd take care of any dogs he had in a nicer way."

She bugged her eyes. "Oh, I know!" she said. "Isn't it a crime? I said something once, and I nearly lost all my visitation privileges with my grandkids. It's just wrong, what he does with those pups. I keep Murphy away from him."

"And he probably thinks that you spoil Murphy."

She had brought her coffee cup up to her shiny lips, then put the cup down again to say, "Did he say that?"

"No, no. He just probably would."

"Probably."

Tristan wanted to talk about Mr. Jimenez some more. "He seems to be an okay dad." He was still talking about Earl, but he'd learned from his experience as a teacher that he could often steer a conversation the way he wanted it without seeming to, so that he could make a point. It was sort of like a Platonic dialogue, only more underhanded.

Mrs. Jimenez put her palm down flat next to her silverware as if to hold the table steady. "Well, yes, but talk about spoiling. Do you know how old his youngest is, and still he runs around with a pacifier? And he's a bed wetter. I can't have him stay with me overnight because I have guests to think of."

"Were you and Mr. Jimenez tough cookies, parentwise?"

"Well. We weren't monsters. Is that what Joe told you? I'll bet that's what he said. The Lord knows what Joe told you."

"It's a son's job to rebel," Tristan said, but that wasn't going to be enough, so he said, "He loved you. Didn't he leave you all that money?" Inwardly, he winced. He wished he hadn't said it. It not only led away from Mr. Jimenez, but it made him sound jealous and made her know she'd been talked about behind her back. Also, he did not want to seem weak, he would not allow her to know that the money was important to him. She could not, at least, have that.

But he couldn't have anticipated that these were the right things to say, and in the right combination. "Yes—it's very good of him. He knew that he was the man of the house and he had a responsibility to take care of me. I know it's an old-fashioned idea, but I'm an old-fashioned girl. He provided for me even better than his father did. Not that his father was a failure. He was just so unfinished, so full of potential."

Mrs. Jimenez pulled a small wicker basket full of colored Easter eggs close to herself and gently rolled one over the fruit-patterned oilcloth. Her nail polish color, he realized, deserved to be called something more particular than candy apple. It was a shade that might have shown at the bottom of one of those paint sample strips as "Cabaret" or "Heartbreak." Probably, like the paint on her house, it dried a shade darker than she anticipated. It was a bolder, firmer version of the color of the egg in her hand, which might have shown up on the other end of the paint sample grade as "Sugar Daddy" or "Wedding Cake."

The eggshell became a web of breaks, and with alacrity, she peeled it off in nearly one piece. It lay at the side of her plate like some Easter gecko's shed skin. She took one big bite out of the hardboiled egg after salting it, and the bold yolk was a perfect revealed circle.

"That's one advantage of knowing you're going to die," said Tristan. "You can wrap things up in a neat bundle."

"You'd think I'd learn a lesson, wouldn't you?" She refilled Tristan's coffee cup. "But having a son die makes me feel immortal. I'm just going to go on and on, I've decided. Nobody there to inherit anything."

"There's Maria!"

"She doesn't like my taste. She'll sell everything off the second I go."

"She'd make a great innkeeper. But we're talking like you're dying. You're a healthy woman, Mrs. Jimenez."

She smiled. "So are you!" she said, and patted his belly, *el panzón.* "Very healthy."

Tristan groaned. "I'm fat, aren't I? Everybody says I look healthy, but what they mean is, I'm fat." He went to make Santa Clausy jolly belly pats with his hands, and knocked over the full cup of coffee into his lap. Since he was only wearing a robe, it scalded his leg terribly. "Yah!" he yelled and stood up. Had she seen his privates? Who cared, he was burning.

"Poor dear." She was up in a flash, hustling him into the bathroom. She drew water in the tub and put her wrist under the tap as she would to gauge the temperature for an infant's bath. "You hop in the shower and I'll clean up the table." The table was a swamp of coffee across the oilcloth. "Hop in," she coaxed.

He dropped his robe on the floor and slipped behind the shower curtain when she left momentarily to sop up. He heard her yell,

"Get away, Murph!" The bathroom door was still wide open, but he was safe behind the opaque shower curtain. The spot on his leg where the coffee spilled was as pink as the egg Mrs. Jimenez had peeled. Not Sugar Daddy, but Peppermint.

He heard her reenter the bathroom. Did she want to get an eyeful? "Here, honey, I know how much you like coffee." She'd brought a fresh cup and placed it near the soap dish on the rim of the bathtub. "Careful, it's full."

She kept talking to him while he showered. Since he was in, he might as well soap up. The spray felt good on the burn, a different temperature. "I always tell people how strong you make coffee," she said from around the corner. "When I came to see you that time after Joe died, you used to make that stuff, gads, the spoon stood straight up, *mi vida*. Every once in a while, Maria will make it too strong and I'll say, 'Good Lord, this is Tristan Coffee!' "

Tristan laughed from the shower. Her coffee stank. He reached down to get a drink from the mug anyway.

This time, it was not Tristan's fault. He thought she'd set it firmly in the corner, but it slipped and fell onto the hard floor, and broke. "Mamma mia," Tristan said, and wondered why he said that—it was not a turn of phrase he was known for using. If he'd been at home, however, he would have cussed up a storm.

He poked his head out of the curtain and put a dripping leg out onto the floor, ready to take care of this mess.

She was there in a jiffy. "I can't keep up with you!" she laughed. "You get back in that shower this instant. This is broken sharp stuff and you've got bare feet; don't be silly. I don't know that much first aid. And Murphy, out, out!" She took a moment to sweep up the dog in one hand and she carried him on her shoulder out to the back door, slamming the screen door on the little guy. She came back in with a dishrag.

"Well, I couldn't help noticing you don't have any of those silly tattoos or pierces," she said. "What a nice surprise."

Joe had had two tattoos, one of a compass legend on the back of one calf, another of a bow and arrow over his heart. Sometimes it was easier for Tristan to see those tattoos in his head than it was to see Joe's face. Both his nipples had been pierced, which his mother knew about and hated, and he had a Prince Albert, which she didn't know about but which she probably suspected, since a handful of jewelry had been given to her along with the box of his ashes at the crematorium, and she must have realized that neither of his ears had been pierced. Tristan recalled reading in one of the AIDS newsletters about the problem with infections, and the explicit list of different piercings. He could see Mrs. Jimenez reading about Prince Alberts and having an epiphany.

"I just think these kids who run around tattooed up to their eyeballs have zero imagination," she said. She was piling up the shards of broken coffee mug. "Don't they realize they are cutting off a lot of job opportunities by putting naughty words over their eyelids?"

He heard her carrying the mug remains to the little wastebasket, behind which Joe's rubber scorpion had once terrified him. She dropped the mess in.

"What's this?" he heard her say.

When he thought back on this moment, it had one of those instant replay effects to it, his realizing what she had come across. In his mind, a hundred times he said, Oh God, oh no, Oh God. Something fell out of orbit: it was like a temporal shift on a science fiction movie, or a glitch in a sound system when words don't sync up with a person's lips. When the Scots played bagpipes, he was always puzzled by the way tune and air didn't match, as the piper took breaths and yet the song continued even when his lips were away from the mouthpiece, like biloquism. "What's this?" Mrs. Jimenez had said.

He realized she had found his bottle of pills on the shelf over the sink, which he'd been so careful to pack away before leaving each day. He'd used one of the big monthly protease bottles to carry all of the mix. The words were all over it. Among the many drugstore codes and directives—"Take with food," "By mouth"—the word "NELFINIVIR" was printed clearly in big blue letters.

"What is this?" she asked again.

He turned off the water and stood silently behind the curtain, all the remaining water running down his unpierced, untattooed body. "Can you hand me a towel?" he said, into the shower nozzle.

A painted, bangled brown hand appeared with a thick white towel. He heard her click on her heels back into the dining area, and shut the bathroom door behind her.

He didn't really stall while drying off, but by the time he did, and by the time he'd dressed and slapped out of the bathroom, towel around his neck, she'd laid out in front of her the three different kinds to study. She'd obviously been crying but now had stopped. Murphy was in her lap and she was petting him to death.

Tristan sat down next to her. She'd already poured a third cup and he realized that the gurgling behind him was his personal coffeemaker chugging away on a new batch. There were two of those vacuum packs ripped open and emptied. She'd doubled the strength just for him. He took a grateful sip and put the cup down. He pulled both hands away as if he'd managed to put the second floor onto a house of cards and it still hadn't collapsed. "So far, so good!" he said.

"So this is what they look like," she said. "I thought they'd be white. But they're blue, baby blue. How do they taste?"

"I try not to taste them. They dissolve really quickly. It tastes like a nasty powder, is all."

"Joe gave it to you, didn't he?" she said.

He hated that question. He thought of the broken glass in his suitcase and hated that it was in there. Who cares who broke it: the fact is, it's broken.

What gave Tristan HIV? Effectively, Joe did. Tristan had been blinded by the magician's magic and couldn't see beyond the smoke and mirrors of his lovable existence. Sure, there was skanky Jesús somewhere in Nogales, but could Tristan blame him? Would anybody on earth believe him if he said that what gave him HIV was that time he came to visit Joe on a worksite and he found the love of his life sitting high on a ladder, with a metal electric box in one hand and a screwdriver in the other, lost utterly to the love of his own work, his ego dissolved in the pleasure of making electricity flow? Oh, how beautiful and lovable people are, thought Tristan, when they are doing what they love to do.

But Joe didn't give it to Tristan single-handedly.

"Didn't he?" she pressed.

"No."

"All that time, then, you've been keeping it from me. So I wouldn't worry?"

When Joe had finally decided to tell his mother that he'd been sick, it was on the occasion of their third visit to Tucson when the lesions had begun to show on his neck and the nagging cough never left. Tristan had pressed Joe to tell her. The way air-conditioning worked on Joe's respiratory system or sinus cavities or whatever seemed to make everything worse, drying him out, plugging him up. "You've got to tell her that she needs to turn off all the air-conditioning, or we can't stay with her. You've got to tell her why."

When they arrived and found the city in a summer heat wave (their plane home would be delayed because it was too hot to get lift), his mother was waiting in what she called an *estufa,* an oven, and she was sweaty, bitchy, *estufado,* and miraculously clueless. "Is this some new religion you're practicing?" she asked, fanning herself.

She asked this because her daughter had gone Pentecostal and stopped doing any kind of work on a Saturday night, gave up beer. "Have you become Amish or something?" And then he told her, with Tristan sitting right beside him.

She didn't break down at first. In fact, she wouldn't, weirdly, talk to her son directly, but threw a dozen questions at Tristan, as if he were the doctor, or the cult leader who had converted her son. Or seroconverted him.

"How about you?" she asked. "Are you sick too?"

"No, Mom, Tristan's negative."

She screwed up her eyes. "Then don't you feel like you're in danger? Aren't you afraid?"

"I love him." They assured her that they knew what they were doing, that they were careful. Being careful, Mrs. Jimenez must have believed, was celibacy. That she could not imagine Joe and Tristan having sex together perhaps hastened her acceptance of their partnership. Nurse-and-patient was a relationship easier for her to imagine.

Now she sat here, and Murphy looked ready to escape her love at the first possible chance. "Did you have it all along?"

Tristan said, "I didn't give it to Joe."

"Then what? You've been carrying this around all these years and you didn't tell me?"

"I haven't told anybody," he said, and this was the honest truth. Only his doctor and the pharmacist in his neighborhood.

"Your mother doesn't know? Do you think you're a hero by not telling anybody?"

Tristan dropped his forehead to the oilcloth. "I am only ashamed. It's so uninteresting, I think, shame." Unromantic.

"Did you hide it even from Joe?" she pressed.

Tristan shook his head. "I didn't know I had it when Joe was alive."

"You got it after he died? After all you knew about it?"

Tristan shrugged. He reached over for the pills lined up in front of her, and took his dosage, washed down with hot coffee.

Then he said, "You have got to make one promise. You've got to swear on a stack of Bibles."

"Swear what?" Mrs. Jimenez, he could tell, took vows seriously.

"That you can't ever tell anybody."

"Why not?"

"Because nobody can know. I want it to be nonexistent as much as it can be. I want it never to see the light of day. I won't give this thing an ounce of attention it doesn't deserve." Only magicians could cast spells on Tristan. Not a shabby little virus. If meds couldn't stave it off, sheer mistreatment and contempt might work, as far as Tristan was concerned.

Mrs. Jimenez had lost so much poise she'd grabbed her own lips and pulled off a gleaming coat of lipstick. "I don't understand you! If I were you, I'd be yelling it out to the world! I'd tell total strangers."

"It's just not me," he said. It sounded pleasingly double-edged in his mind: that isn't what I'd do, he meant, but it also had a faggier swish to it—It doesn't match my outfit. He noticed how he was femmier around straight people, especially manly men. He flapped his wrists more, squealed. On the other hand, when he was with gay men who affected a swish, he'd counter it with firm maleness. This wasn't phobia or contrariness so much as a desire to give the world balance and variety—with loud people he spoke quietly, and vice versa.

It pleased him, but it didn't please Mrs. Jimenez. "Please, just promise."

"Do you know how much you're asking me? How much this weighs on me?"

Why does it always weigh on people, Tristan wondered. It didn't weigh nearly as much to him. "Please."

She drummed her lipsticky fingers on the oilcloth. She said, "Not even Maria or Mik?"

"Especially not Maria or Mik."

She made him wait. Then she said, "I promise."

Mrs. Jimenez was furious; he could see the hatred even as she served him more coffee. "Why would you do that?" She spoke to him as if she were his girlfriend who had bailed him out of jail on too many occasions, and now he'd fallen victim to the Three-Strikes-You're-Out law. Behind these questions was a statement: I have given you so much and every time I have asked you to end this, make this stop, and this is the way you've chosen to make it end.

Their relationship was ending right before his eyes, ending sloppily. Tristan and Mrs. Jimenez were like two exhausted prize-fighters who, in this penultimate round, had fallen against each other, in order to continue standing, punching lazily; and though a referee pulled them apart now and then, they clung to each other anyway, throwing halfhearted jabs—and all the time, they could easily have been mistaken by the audience for embracing lovers.

21

Mik pulled up about an hour later at the Christmas-colored bed-and-breakfast. Tristan had been sitting by the window and waiting. Mrs. Jimenez had beat a retreat soon after they realized they didn't want to talk to each other anymore. Tristan had fidgeted for an hour, poking around, reading travel brochures and the guest register. When he heard Mik's car pull up he almost ran to it.

He slammed the door and buckled himself in. "I don't want to go back to Old Pascua."

"I thought you wanted to see the rest of the ceremony."

"I do, but not there." He was thinking of Father Dolan. He didn't want any confrontation with him, either. "Why don't we go to the other village, out in the desert. Don't you think it will be more authentic with no freeway overpass distracting us?"

"I've never been there," said Mik.

"I've got a map."

"I know where it is, Tristan. This is the desert. There aren't that many roads."

On the road, Tristan tried to play the question game he'd played with Maria on the way from the Phoenix airport, but Mik didn't like the questions, or prevaricated ("Favorite painter?" "It's against my principles to enjoy figurative art." "Guns or butter?" "Schools." "Jessica Lange, Sigourney Weaver, or Geena Davis?" "Who?"). He is smarter than I am, Tristan thought, but he's Wotan, king of the gods, trapped by his own forbearance and I am the fool hero who has come to release him, hack, slash.

When they pulled up into the parking lot at New Pascua Village, Tristan was completely devastated. He'd had in his mind that this would be the more authentic, more pure of the ceremonies, away from the city and the white people. But there were at least seven tour buses all parked in a row. One was disgorging old white ladies with big hair, all dressed in their Sunday best.

"How is this possible?" Tristan asked Mik.

"Word gets around."

The church and the plaza were pristine. There wasn't that casino sign or the overpass, but oddly, Tristan missed them. There were several sets of bleachers, and people spectating as if at a football game. Over the church flew three flags: in the center, the American flag, the Mexican to the left, and on the right, the Yaqui Nation flag, a blue field with a black cross and a yellow moon in the left corner. Everything looked spiffier, newer, more watched.

All over the ground were bits of confetti, left over from La Gloria the day before. There must have been thousands throwing the stuff, because it was deep even in the outer edges of the village.

"This really stinks," said Tristan.

Mik turned to him. "You know, Tristan, you have to start being more careful about what you say. People can be offended by things you don't think are offensive."

Tristan was in a lousy mood, so he said, "Careful, or more polite?" What was carefulness? Every day, you leave your house to go to work and you remember to lock your door, even though you know locks are for honest people. One day, you're in such a hurry, you forget to lock it up, and you come home after a long day, and you realize what you did, and you are surprised to find that nobody cared, nobody walked with the TV. You start playing with that, you don't lock it on purpose, and sure enough, nobody rips you off. Of course, you don't go trumpeting it around. But life is too short to be careful.

"Earl is really pissed, isn't he?" Tristan said after a few minutes.

Mik sat down in the bleachers, looking like he didn't really want to be with Tristan, his eyes shifting toward other people now and then, hoping not to be recognized. "He heard what you said about his dogs."

It wasn't the fact that Mrs. Jimenez was being a bigmouth about the dogs that scared Tristan, nor the swiftness with which she'd gone off blabbing. It was what else she could be a bigmouth about. But she promised, she made a *manda,* for God's sake.

"Now it's all coming back to me," he said out loud. "Small town life. Everybody knows everybody else's business. Doesn't anybody have enough going on in their lives that there's not something else to talk about?"

"I think Maria believes there's only one bigmouth in town right now," Mik said. "Look, the head Pascola."

One of the men dressed in an oval mask with a long, long beard came up front after executing a few particular but unmetered steps. He was apologizing about something. "Maybe they're sorry the Chapayekas tried to rape Maria."

"Shh," Mik said.

A group of Deer Singers came out and sang, and Tristan wished he had Refugio here to translate for him. He felt oddly protected by Refugio. At Maria's house, he had gone to the bathroom during dinner the evening before, and passed a bedroom in the hall that must have been Earl's father's. Each leg of the bed frame rested in the basin of a bowl filled with water. "To protect him from scorpions," Maria said, and did a muted version of the eye roll so she wouldn't cause trouble.

What we white people want, Tristan decided, is some belief that we've prepared for every eventuality, and kept our fate from getting too close to us. Preventative procedures. Tristan thought this, and it led him to recall that he hadn't been to see a dentist in almost five years.

The Deer Dancer came out and danced inside the pattern of a cross on the ground. The singers sang around him and poured more cross shapes into the dust with water from the basin in which the drum had floated.

The Fariseos were back, but they were transformed. They carried switches of cottonwood and had twigs of cottonwood in their hats.

"That Deer Dancer isn't as good as the one at Old Pascua," Tristan told Mik.

"He's young; he's learning."

Tristan squinted his eyes. He must be going blind. The Deer Dancer was a kid! How could that be? The Deer Dancer had to be old, for him, a symbol of wisdom and innocence all rolled in one little package. Tristan felt a weird outrage. "Let's get closer," he said.

The dance was short and colorful, and there was, distastefully, applause after he finished. There'd been no applause at Old Pascua.

"Their obligations are finished," said Mik. Now they can entertain the crowds. They had indeed moved to the side of the church and let the church group fuss with the altar. There were two Chapayekas who still had their masks, unburned in La Gloria's bonfire. They wore them on the backs of their heads.

Tristan went up to the Deer Dancer to get a closer look. Yes, he really was young, as young as Refugio, maybe. He was meatless, though, all bones and growth spurt, a Deer Dancer for the future, for the twenty-first century. The best way to prepare for the next millennium, as far as Tristan was concerned, was not to prepare.

"Got a cigarette?" the Deer Dancer—the fawn dancer—asked Tristan, who'd been staring and hadn't realized it.

"Cigarette?" He knew it was traditional to give Deer Dancers cigarettes (for energy), but this seemed more like giving cigarettes to a minor, probably because it was. Tristan wasn't going to be an enabler, not any more, not drugwise, not religionwise.

Once on a late Saturday afternoon, he'd been walking to his favorite Chinese vegetarian restaurant in the avenues, and an Orthodox Jew in his hat and glasses and earlocks had buttonholed Tristan. "Will you come with me, please," he said, more a directive than a query. Tristan walked behind him for several blocks, out of the business strip and into residential stucco houses.

They came to one that was blue and well-kept, the front door of which stood wide open. Tristan followed the Jew up the stairs and into the house and feared some kind of ambush, until he saw a woman with a little boy sitting in the front room, and she smiled and said, "Oh, good," when he passed by.

But they kept walking deeper into the house, down a long habittrail corridor. There were no pictures on the walls. Tristan knew enough about Orthodox Judaism to know that they followed the Ten Commandments pretty closely, which forbade graven images (couldn't they make an exception for Titian?) and that this man he was following woke up every morning and said, "Thank God I was not born a woman."

There was a sound coming from the back of the house—what was it? A car alarm from down the street? An unpleasant musical instrument? No, an alarm clock, or smoke detector, something sustained and maddening.

They came into the kitchen. The man pointed at the stove. "Will you please turn that off?" he asked. The oven timer had gone off, and since it was the Sabbath, he could not allow himself to turn it off. Tristan walked over and, the Sabbath goy, turned the handle with one quick twist.

The man sighed as if Tristan had defused a bomb. "Thank you."

"Anything else?"

The Jew thanked Tristan for the offer. "Could you move that chair over there? And open that window a crack?"

Tristan cheerfully went at these tasks. "I don't do windows," he reminded the man.

The man laughed. At least in San Francisco, they liked Tristan's sense of humor. "Thank you. There's some matzoh on top of the refrigerator if you'd like some."

"That's okay." And Tristan went on his way. Weren't goyim forbidden to walk into a kosher kitchen?

He'd helped Joe into heaven by forcing upon him a priest's last rites. He'd eaten one dish at a time with Muslim Mik at the table. But no more. He could see in Mik here how such obligations led to tougher stuff, untenable fundamentalism. Fundamentalism was not so troubling to Tristan as a source of intolerance as it was a method of building fences that kept people in and out of a person's world.

No cigarettes, then, for the jailbait Deer Dancer.

From behind him, Mik offered the kid a Camel. "Thanks, man."

The boy smoked like he was born smoking. Tristan whipped out his wallet, and pulled out the prayer card of Jesús Malverde, the one given him years before by Jesús, the Nogales prostitute. He showed it to the boy. The boy lit up with recognition.

The boy eagerly reached for his own wallet, hidden behind the shawl in his rolled-up pants. He pulled out his own prayer card, the same size as Tristan's, but different. It showed Malverde with his hands bound behind his back with a noose hanging behind him, thrown over a tree branch. A patch of cattails grew on his left. "Robin Hood," said the Deer Dancer, smiling. On the back was the prayer: "Today prostrate before your cross oh Malverde my Lord I beg of you mercy and that you relieve my pain." At the bottom, this card had directions: Make the petition and pray 3 Our Fathers and 3 Hail Marys. Light two candles. Carry an amulet or the lodestone, mostly red.

Somebody called the boy and he ran off, just like that, before Tristan could ask him any questions.

Tristan said to Mik, "Is this it? Because if all this is today is one big fiesta, I've seen enough. Isn't there some place we can go to get some souvenirs? I need a new oilcloth. Where can we get oilcloth? The one I have at home is gummy."

Mik said, "All right, let's go."

They had to make a stray Mexican dog move from behind their tires, because it was nice and shady there. Tristan tried to make him move with his hands against the dog's rump, but Mik just pushed it roughly with his foot, and it got right up.

They pulled out onto the road. In this direction, the ground was flat, limitless. The future spread out before Tristan with endless cycles of prescription renewals, blood workups, and checkups. And that was Tristan's fundamentalism, the fence that kept him from all of these other people, the necessity, the religion, the culture of his viral condition. It could be criticized the way a Muslim fatwa could, or a Pentecostal restriction on blood transfusions, or the killing of a toro in the bullfights.

The last portion of the bullfights was called "The Third of the Death."

22

Mik told Tristan he'd take him to Saguaro State Park, but first they should go to the old Mission San Xavier, since it was so close. On the map, it was squared off the way forbidden missile range zones were.

San Xavier was a churrigueresque confection newly white-washed and recently restored, so that the frescos inside were bold and fresh. Even though it was Easter Sunday, there were very few people, a complete contrast to the touristy New Pascua Village.

There was a small chapel to the side, a gussied-up version of the Yaqui churches. The chapel was banked with votive candles. The shape of the room made Tristan feel like he'd stepped into a kiln. He had an odd respect for the cultures of this region, always going one more step to make an already hot and austere way of life just that much more so: salsa, salditos, chiles, candles. There were more air conditioners in Michigan, he'd bet.

Inside was a wooden statue of San Xavier reclined on a bench, wood on wood, giving the impression of discomfort. The old wooden man was draped in a robe and was perhaps a recycled cru-cified Christ or lesser religious figure, festooned here with peti-tions, there with notes of thanks, Easter lilies, and photographs.

"Do you know the legend?" Tristan asked Mik.

"Remind me."

"If you have a request for the saint, you have to come here and lift his head. Only the faithful are able to lift his head."

"You're kidding," said Mik. "How difficult could it be?"

Tristan shrugged. "Probably it's a psychosomatic thing. People who feel guilty or unworthy are going to let their superegos stop them."

Tristan wished he were like that. He could pass lie detector tests—he had—telling whoppers while remaining as cool as a cucumber. He walked over to the head end of the saint and cradled it between his hands. He was impressed by the smoothness of the wood underneath, around the crown, worn down by thousands of gentle hands. He told Mik about it. "You know, I don't know how much I believe, or how much you believe," he said, "but you just have to be impressed when you feel the head of a saint all worn down like that. Grooves in church steps from people climbing up on their knees. All those candles." And what remains when disbelief has gone, the poet asks. Tristan made a motion like he was going to attempt to lift.

Mik said, "It doesn't really matter if you don't have a petition."

With not a little relief, Tristan let go without trying. "All these petitions," he said, walking back over to Mik. "Is that the only reason people pray anymore? Because they want something? Is God just a Santa Claus for adults?"

Mik had fished out four quarters from his pocket and was feeding them into a little black bank, which allowed him to light a votive candle. "Why do you pray?" he asked.

Tristan watched him get on his knees. On the wall behind the candles were dozens of religious pictures painted on glass, backed by crushed tin foil, a folk art he'd learned himself at summer camp when he was twelve. "I say thank you," Tristan said, "but I don't pray very much. Mostly I read. I swim laps. Stare at the ocean."

"California," said Mik. "Pshh."

Tristan would have made a retort but he wanted to watch Mik. Was he going to cross himself now?

But he just got up and the two of them left the chapel for the parking lot. Mik said, "I suppose you thought it was funny to watch a Muslim light a Catholic candle."

"No, I just thought it was very Californian of you."

When Joe had died, Tristan had attended the Catholic funeral, but he'd also, with several Buddhist friends, had a peaceful funeral in that tradition, which involved him taking a bit of food and drink that was meant to be a meal for the dead, as well as the ashes of a burned photograph of Joe, up to the top of a high hill in San Francisco and casting it widely. It was a windy day then, and the drink blew back onto him. It was champagne.

"I do it for Joe," said Mik. "He was Catholic. It's like speaking a foreign language when you're in another country." They got in the car and pulled away. Mik said, "It's strange, you know, I never observed Ramadan when I lived with my parents. All that fasting and whatever. But since they moved away, I observe it . . . religiously."

It made sense. When a person left home, a person tended to cling closely to whatever could be salvaged from home—religion flourished because of emigration.

"Of course, it's easy to fast during the daylight these years, in the winter, when sunrise and sunset are so close together. Basically all it is is skipping lunch."

"You know, Joe wasn't that religious. I think you should know that," said Tristan. He thought, I was the one up in the bedroom every night saying fucking novenas. "When I called in a priest to give last rites, he kinda hit the roof."

Conversation between the two of them began to lurch crazily, when it went at all. They parked the car in silence.

In the state park, there were a half dozen hikes they could have taken, but Mik knew one that had a wide variety of plants and wildlife that Tristan might not have seen before. In his glove compartment, he had the beat-up Audubon guidebook called *Deserts*. He handed it to Tristan, and Tristan flipped through. Sprigs and blossoms were pressed between the pages. Since it was Easter morning, there were no other cars parked in the lot at the trailhead—everybody was at church. Here was Tristan with a Muslim on the day of Christ's Resurrection. It was on holidays that being un-Christian or un-straight was most obvious. Holidays were for family; maybe that was all holidays were really for. When Tristan got angry at his own Catholicism, it was usually during weddings, where he sulked conspicuously. Truly, he thought that all those pieces of willowware they'd received at their own domestic partnership seemed silly, unimaginative.

"Have you gone to Mecca?" Tristan asked Mik, as they stepped around the "No dogs" sign.

"Yes, I've gone. What brought that up?"

The sky was a starched cloudless blue. Five big hawks wheeled, looking both gay and fierce.

"I've been thinking about pilgrimage," said Tristan. "Going to Jerusalem, Mecca, whatever. It's something we do. Coming here is a kind of pilgrimage for me. To see Joe."

"What does it feel like?" Mik pointed at a brittle bush, all in flower, just like the one at the cemetery. "People come to see saints on pilgrimages all the time. Look how red the ocotillo is."

"Did you go to Mecca?" Tristan asked again. He recalled Mister Wizard's pure white clothes.

"Yes, it was wonderful." But no matter how many times Tristan pressed with more particular questions, Mik didn't give him colorful details except one: that since everybody was wearing the same outfit, nobody could tell whether you were rich or poor. Mik ended the conversation with a gentle but firm: "I think one of the greatest aspects of pilgrimage is the personal and private one."

Tristan blushed and apologized. Mik didn't say, oh, that's okay, which probably meant that an apology had been necessary. Or Mik had not heard him, hopping from rock to rock down the trail.

They crossed a hill and came upon a spectacular view of hundreds of saguaros. They looked like people, mothers with children, aged men, giant heroes, strolling among the bramble.

"Charles came on pilgrimage, I see," said Tristan.

Mik stopped suddenly. "Did Mrs. Jimenez tell you?" He seemed surprised.

"I read his entry in the guest book in my room." Tristan had been flipping through the guest register full of effusive thanks: "We had a blast!" "Henry brung a ring, and Betsy said sure, you betcha." "Red and green are perfect, because it's Christmas here every day!" Or simply, "The Bartletts, Sandusky, Ohio." Tristan had been trying to think of something witty and kind to put on a page when he came across Charles' greetings: "Happy New Year to my second family, and Murphy, the wonder dog!" Tristan flipped to the beginning of the book and found a previous entry on the previous new year. Charles called Murphy the wonder dog there, too. Tristan decided not to sign himself.

"You act like I'm not supposed to know," he said to Mik. "Why are you hiding his visits?"

Mik was scrutinizing the buds on a teddy bear cholla. Little balls of the spiny plant pulled off easily, sticking to animals or people and taking root somewhere else. Mik was trying hard, Tristan thought, not to make a big deal of this, but he could see the strain. "Charles said that you and he didn't get along. He said you were angry with him."

Tristan sputtered. "Angry? What an egomaniac. Even *nothing* is something to Charles. Jesus, Mik, it's not like that. When I'm angry with somebody, it's usually because they matter. Charles doesn't matter to me. I don't even know where Charles is. I don't know what he does."

Mik said, "He's in San Francisco in the house he always lived in. He plans catering events in a fancy hotel."

Tristan had never been to Charles's house the whole time he and Joe were together. "I guess you're pretty close to him," Tristan said, not really wanting to know the answer to that. A lizard darted out of the cholla they'd both leaned forward to inspect. Tristan was startled and pulled back, and his sock brushed against another cholla behind him. Pulling the barbed needles out of the material proved a messy and pointy task. "God, I'm getting worse and worse," Tristan complained, and he realized that Mik might interpret this statement as relating to his feelings about Charles, not his clumsiness in the desert.

Mik waited but didn't help. Tristan said, "Do you think it's possible that I need to get my eyes examined, that my sight has something to do with all my clumsy accidents? Or an inner-ear imbalance? Do you think people's motor skills get worse when they get older?"

Mik was austere, simple in his anger. "Maybe you're just careless," he said, and Tristan heard the two words in one: care, less.

"Why do I have to be friends with Charles? What kind of dishonor to Joe is my not keeping in touch with Charles?"

Mik said, "You could have thanked him for everything he did. You could have given him a knife or a jacket or something."

"You know, Mik, he was more trouble than help. We could have had day nurses and night nurses, but he wanted to do it during the day, and I let him. He was alone with Joe more than I ever got to be for the last half year. Every night I'd come home and Joe'd be asleep, or need to be fed or washed, and all these people would come to make their fucking pilgrimage to see dear saintly Joe and guess who got to entertain them, and talk to them, and chase them out when he got tired? Joe sent them all home—especially Charles—with hundreds of little mementos every day. Christ, I let him write the fucking obituary, and organize the memorial."

"Charles said you wouldn't do it, so he had to."

"He said that?"

Mik shrugged. "You won't make a quilt panel. And Chow-Chow said you wouldn't let him make the pilgrimage. So-called."

"Chow-Chow? That asshole? What, is he coming down here too?"

"You didn't see his name in the book? Right next to Charles's?"

"If he didn't sign it 'Chow-Chow,' then I wouldn't recognize it. I don't even know his real name."

"It's Martin. Anyway, why didn't you let Martin see Joe just before he died?"

"That fucker never bothered!" Tristan was screaming, stomping. The silent desert made him sound even louder, and crazy. "He'd float into town in one of those stupid-fuck cars of his and call us from the car phone to tell us he was coming for dinner. Joe would spend hours cooking and then we'd get another call and he'd tell us he'd met some boy or, even more offensive, he'd lie and tell us he was lost, and he never showed. Mik, in four years, all that time, I never even met that flaky-assed shithead."

Mik made a tisking sound. Tristan wanted to scream at him, too. This desert, Mik, this tragedy, all of it has made you a dry, tragic, moral monster. You are brittle, Mik, and prideful and arrogant. You are just the opposite of me, shameful and soft and spineless me, but we are just two sides of the same counterfeit coin, a plug nickel pulled by the magician from behind a volunteer's ear.

"I don't know who to believe," Mik said. "Charles and Chow-Chow come once a year to see Joe's grave. This is your first time. They seem much more affected."

"You think that I don't care? *I* don't care? You don't even care whether your parents named the fucking pet monkey. Hey, Monkey, my ass."

"It wasn't really a pet, you know. They didn't go down to the animal shelter and pick him up. They just put monkey chow or something out for it once and now it just stays. It hasn't had any shots or anything. They're not cute, monkeys, not there. Scaggy."

"Oh, I don't give a damn about the stupid monkey."

They'd come abruptly to the end of the trail, which was a cliff with a sign-board panorama silhouette naming the various peaks in the distance. These ranges were high, but brief and scalped, the view in the distance of a place that for once, Tristan did not want to go.

"Christ, it's like some sort of conspiracy," said Tristan. "You've got no idea how much I cared about Joe. You've got none. It's a *private* fucking pilgrimage."

"Calm down, Tristan," said Mik.

"Let me explain how I feel now, Mik. Let me make it clear. Let me tell you, for instance, how Chow-Chow didn't come on that last day, how that happened."

On the Friday before he died, there'd been nothing but exhaustion, all those friends and the priest Joe had resented ("There ARE atheists in foxholes," he screeched at the confused man from St. Kevin's), the lovely chiropractor, the Latino queen from Shanti who chickaboomed through a hebdomadal (Shanti's fact-sheet word) bathroom cleaning, the social worker with her forms, Charles and his washrag compresses, and then, yet again, the phone call from Chow-Chow, cruising the city, deciding he had to come over.

"Chow-Chow, I'm sorry," Tristan had said. "But it's ten o'clock and Joe's asleep and I'm exhausted. Are you in town all weekend? Come tomorrow; you can sit all day with him tomorrow."

But Chow-Chow didn't come on Saturday, nor did he call. And Sunday, no sign. But on that Monday, after the squeaky-voiced giant coroner with his weight belt for picking up bodies, and the Superfly assistant, and the policewoman who said she liked poetry, and the white van that was just like Joe's old Thumper, after all of them had come and gone, then Chow-Chow called from his

stupid cellular phone to ask if he could come see Joe now, before
he headed back to Reno, and Tristan had just laughed, howled, and
had to say twice, because Chow-Chow had gone into a tunnel and
lost the signal when Tristan said it the first time: "No, you can't,
because he's dead." (There'd been fun in telling telemarketers and
creditors the same thing: Sorry, he can't come to the phone right
now, he's quite dead.)

"They wouldn't let me close Joe's bank account. I had no right,"
he told Mik. "His mother got a small fortune from his life insurance. For four years I was paying his health insurance premiums
out of my own pocket! I was taking care of him. When he was in a
bad mood, I had to put up with it." It was all coming out of him,
like the sick that came from a lanced sore.

Tristan remembered Joe walking through the house, with fluid
on his brain, thinking he was going through his normal routine, but
banging into walls and missing door handles like a drunk. He'd
snap at Tristan and refuse to take his meds.

"You could have called us. We would have come and helped."
Mik tossed something into his mouth. Did he have food? Why
didn't he offer Tristan some?

"Helped? I've seen the way folks in Tucson take care of dogs—
or monkeys, for that matter—and I wouldn't put a human in your
hands."

Mik stopped him. If he decided to hit Tristan, Tristan wouldn't
know what to do. But the rage was running its course. Tristan was
nursing it. It felt hard-wired, something that couldn't be stopped
by anything but a deeply radical, miraculous thing, like logic or
sleep. His speech was filigreed with all the wrong that had been
done to him, and he clutched this toxic lacework as if it were spun
from gold thread. Wind blew up around them and blew dust in
Tristan's eyes and teeth. That was just fucking perfect.

Mik tossed more of something into his mouth. Tristan the
teacher wanted to say, "Have you got enough to share with the rest
of the class?"

Mik said, "How do you know what those dogs like? Dogs hate
to be alone. The worst thing you can do to a dog is leave it alone,
without its pack."

Tristan did not want to talk about dogs, or monkeys, and yet here they were, only talking about dogs and monkeys. Tristan thought about the Murphster, out in this desert.

But it struck him that Mik was not talking about dogs at all, but about his failure to be true to Charles and Chow-Chow, and by association, to Joe.

Mik looked at him intensely, that unknown look that dogs give when you think you have both sussed each other out, and that it's safe to reach out and pat the dog on the head, just before the lunge and the hand is bitten off. Mik gave him that look, but for once, sloppy Tristan recognized it. He was always making mistakes, yet somehow, they were never quite fatal, even when they ought to be.

Mik slammed something more into his mouth, perhaps as a gobstopper, so he wouldn't leak any more poison.

"What are you eating?" Tristan demanded.

"Salditos. Want one?"

Sour salted plums. You biddy, Tristan thought, you parsimonious fundamentalist living dead.

"I have one more thing to say to you, Mik, and then you'll take me home." He said that to make sure Mik knew that he was not allowed to leave him out in the open, sleeping under a saguaro, peeing dried crystals like a kangaroo rat. "I can't be a blank slate; I can't worship Joe. I loved him—more than you'll ever know. But I can't be religious about it like you, Mik."

"You're just lazy," Mik said, dismissing him. "No rigor. Self-indulgent. Clumsy."

What could he say to that? "I know you, Mik. You are of this desert place even though you say you're an outsider. But you've done exactly what this desert does. You bloomed all at once like a century plant and then it killed you."

 23

Mik drove off from the B and B without that courtesy idle everybody knows to perform: As the person decarring goes to the door, slips his key into the lock, turns and waves, it's okay; I'm able to get out of these harsh elements. By hitting the gas the moment Tristan stepped out, Mik was saying: you're on your own; you are leaving the Land of the Dead.

Tristan would be lying if he said he wasn't pissed. He felt he'd completely misassessed Mik. What had seemed calm, tolerant observance was in fact soreheadedness, grudge, imperious jealousy. Half the scorn Tristan felt in such instances was fueled by humiliation for a faulty reckoning.

In some ways, the break with Mik was more vivid and central than his riff with Maria, or Mrs. Jimenez. After all, he had once thought Joe and Mik were old lovers. Mik and he were supposed to be outsiders together, of one mind.

When he stepped into the adobe, he found Mrs. Jimenez waiting, sitting on his bed. How long had she been sitting there? Had she spied out the window watching for Mik's arrival, or had there been a conspiracy between the two?

Tristan couldn't tell what the inscrutable stony face was for. Concern? Fury? He realized that her makeup was used not to highlight or reveal emotions but to mask them. She'd become expressionless, or stylized into an untranslatable expression in an Asian drawing or a Greek urn. Her face had thickened into a wall, acceptable—even preferable—socially as pretty, the way porcelain dolls were, or Lalique crystal.

"Hello," he said, trying to glaze over, himself. He didn't want to return to their earlier conversation; perhaps the biggest reason he never told people about his HIV status was because he had no patience for emotional catch-up. He'd spent years getting to this point, and didn't want to take somebody as frail as Mrs. Jimenez by the hand and lead her through the Kübler-Ross stages all over again. At school, he was a teacher who never repeated himself; always he assigned new readings to keep himself from being bored, even if it meant more work for him. "Is there something wrong?" he asked.

He tried to predict how her expression would change, but it didn't. Just what he'd thought he wanted, he was now afraid of: that she was through with him. His mind flashed in a silly way on the sack full of broken drinking glass squirreled away in his suitcase. Had she found it?

"I'm afraid so," she said, and sighed in a businesslike way. She reached from behind herself and pulled out Tristan's plastic bottle that held all his pills. There was a huge hole chewed into it, the Murphster's mouthwork. It was empty. "It must have fallen off the shelf, because he's too small to knock it off himself."

"He ate the pills?" he said.

Then her mask broke, as if rehearsed. "Yes, most of them." And she began to cry, just as he had seen her do at Joe's burial, years before. She didn't reach for Tristan's hand or shoulder, and he stayed decidedly away, too, leaning against the rug on the wall. He felt its coarse woolen weave prickle his neck. She buried her face in an inconvenient posture into the pilly bedspread and made unearthly wailing sounds. Brünnhilde's final aria, as she built the funeral pyre for the one she loved the most, and had killed.

Of course it was impossible that Murphy had done this. But where was the dog; where were his meds?

She looked up after a minute. Her eyes were swollen. Who knew what was faked or felt any more? She clutched the little prayer medallion that had hung with all the other fetishes around Murphy's neck, St. Martin des Porres, patron of lost souls. Hobos, homeless, street trash. *Ruega por nosotros.*

"I took him to the veterinarian's house. Do you remember," she asked, "when he ate all that chocolate? They had to feed him charcoal. They did it again but they don't know if it will do any good.

They must have fallen off the shelf, because he's too small to get them," she repeated.

Was she suggesting he'd put them where the dog would find them? Where had she hidden the dog? Who was helping her hide him? Where were Tristan's pills? How long before it was appropriate for him to say awfully, selfishly, "Where are my pills?"

"There, there," he said.

He had another ghastly thought: what if she had put Murphy down just for the purposes of this episode? To get rid of him? What if Murphy was genuinely dead or dying, fed toxic medicines that looked, for all the world, as if they had been carelessly left behind by a clumsy, absent-minded Tristan? After all the work and money she'd put into Murphy, would she sacrifice him to help expel Tristan from her life? It was so possible. And it was so unnecessarily costly: Tristan would have gone, surely, for free.

Tristan sat next to her on the bed and he cried, too, a lip-biting tear-squeezing cry just thinking of a truly dead Murphy. That desert rat. He put his hand on top of Mrs. Jimenez's for several minutes and they stared ahead like airplane passengers trying to ignore a very bumpy turbulence.

Then Tristan decided to say, "I'm so sorry I left them lying around." And he almost convinced himself then of this possibility. Murphy had chewed things up before. Murphy would eat anything.

He continued, standing up. "But like I told you, I can't last long without those pills."

It was Easter Sunday. The pharmacies would be closed. So would the doctors' offices. He'd feel foolish hitting a hospital emergency room. That Mrs. Jimenez didn't suggest or insist upon it meant that she wanted him to take the standby shuttle home.

24

The final punishment involved taking a bus, alone, to the Phoenix airport. He hated buses. The dust and grime were ineffectively masked by some orangey disinfectant smell. Huge unavoidable windows were meant to afford grand views but only bleached a body with direct headachy sun, sun without its proper benefits. At his right arm, cold air hissed out and the bar of steel trim where he leaned was ice cold, while the rest of his body went on sweating.

Nobody could or would take Tristan to the airport. Mrs. Jimenez was a mess and had to take care of Murphy. Would he survive? Mik was not an option. And Maria and Earl had taken the kids and Earl's dad to a cousin's house to celebrate Easter.

Tristan packed swiftly and dropped the keys to his adobe unit into Mrs. Jimenez's mailbox, as she generally instructed all her paying customers. He didn't leave a note and didn't want to intrude on her troubles, or catch her in a lie, Murphy dozing on her lap. He carried his own heavy suitcase to the bus terminal several blocks away.

Then why did he feel better, anyway? He did feel better, as if he'd been very sick for a long time, but now, for the first time in days, was able to eat a thin soup. There was a sound of feeling better, a song sung in a minor mode, sung gingerly, or like the first time in the Michigan spring when it was warm enough to go barefoot but the feet had yet to toughen.

Even though there were plenty of seats open in the back of the bus, a skinny plain girl who said, among many things, that her name was Tammy and this was her first big trip ever, sat down next to him. He gave her no encouragement; he stared out the window.

Everybody who brought reading material onto the bus brought trashy novels or junky magazines. Tammy, who was a waitress at a department store's lunch counter, was telling him that she'd decided to leave on Easter Sunday because on this day everything was new in the world. She seemed to have fallen for Tristan.

Wrong guy, he warned her in his head. Way wrong, hilariously wrong. If she only knew, she would have brought the story of it back home to friends as the first big adventure on her first big trip.

The driver had idiotically stopped in front of a golf course to count tickets. It was a golf course, or the entrance to some gated community, acres of green grass in the desert. Tristan had to dig around in his pants pockets, which at this point resembled dopey Norman Rockwellish schoolboy's dungarees full of frogs, slingshots, marbles, and Indian-head wooden nickels. Tristan pulled out the little medallion that had hung around Murphy's neck, the receipt from a bookstore, a prayer card of Jesús Malverde, and—he'd forgotten—wrapped in a baggy, the saldito he'd bought with Mik on Good Friday. Two teeth marks marred its asteroidlike perfection. He popped the whole thing in his mouth. It was still horrible, but he refused to spit it out.

"Teekets, pliss," said the driver, only eight rows away. Among all that crap, Tristan couldn't find his ticket stub anywhere. Would the driver throw him off? Even out here, in the middle of the Sonoran desert? In the middle of a golf course in the Sonoran desert? He thought of Murphy, on the side of the road, scrounging for grubs.

He had to get back home. If Tammy weren't such a chatterbox, he was sure he would be able to hear the virus mutating around the drugs he wasn't getting. Oh, it was the stress, he thought, as he searched the other pants pocket and found his Yaqui rosary with its wooden beads. Stress that made his teeth loosen in his gumline, gave him acne, and even made the spot on his arms ache where he got inoculations.

Was the ticket beneath his feet? Did he have enough cash to pay a second time, or would they accept a credit card? How stupid to feel guilty about a wrongdoing he'd never committed. His head was between his own legs like a fainter, his palms to the waxy bus floor. If he stayed like this, would anybody notice him?

Everything was going to be all right, he decided down there, where he could pretend he didn't hear Tammy wanting to know if she could help.

"Are you trying to hide, señor?" he could hear the driver saying.

Tristan sat up sheepishly. "No, sir. I just can't find my ticket stub. You aren't going to throw me off, are you?"

The driver laughed. "I remember you getting on. You were the one who tried to give me a cash rayjeester receipt eenstead of your ticket." Of course, Tristan remembered now. He'd embarrassed himself and pulled it away saying, "Oh, no. That won't do, will it?"

Tristan leaned back. "Thank God. I don't know what I'd do if you threw me out here on the golf course."

The driver made a face. "Golf course?" he said, and continued down the aisle checking the rest of the tickets.

Tristan peered out the window. Tammy put her pale friendly hand on his shoulder. "That's a big cemetery, silly," she said, and laughed, and when Tristan didn't laugh along with her, she said, "But it's nice enough to be a golf course, isn't it?"

ABOUT THE AUTHOR

Brian Bouldrey is the author of the novel *The Genius of Desire* (Ballantine, 1993), editor of *Wrestling with the Angel: Faith and Religion in the Lives of Gay Men* (Putnam/Riverhead, 1995), winner of the 1996 Lambda Book Award, and editor of the annual Best American Gay Fiction series (Little, Brown), also a Lammy nominee. He is the founding editor of the *Harrington Gay Men's Fiction Quarterly,* and his fiction and essays have appeared in *Men on Men, Chick for a Day, Genre, TriQuarterly, The Harvard Review, modern words, Zyzzyva, The James White Review, The Sewanee Review, Fourteen Hills,* and *Flesh & the Word.* He is a frequent contributor to the *San Francisco Bay Guardian* and is Associate Editor of the weekly's literature supplement.

He has taught writing in the extension program at the University of California at Berkeley and in Warren Wilson College's MFA program for writers.

Order Your Own Copy of
This Important Book for Your Personal Library!

LOVE, THE MAGICIAN

_____in hardbound at $29.95 (ISBN: 1-56023-993-X)

_____in softbound at $14.95 (ISBN: 1-56023-994-8)

COST OF BOOKS_____

OUTSIDE USA/CANADA/
MEXICO: ADD 20%____

POSTAGE & HANDLING_____
(US: $4.00 for first book & $1.50
for each additional book)
Outside US: $5.00 for first book
& $2.00 for each additional book)

SUBTOTAL_____

in Canada: add 7% GST____

STATE TAX____
(NY, OH & MIN residents, please
add appropriate local sales tax)

FINAL TOTAL____
(If paying in Canadian funds,
convert using the current
exchange rate, UNESCO
coupons welcome.)

❏ **BILL ME LATER:** ($5 service charge will be added)
(Bill-me option is good on US/Canada/Mexico orders only;
not good to jobbers, wholesalers, or subscription agencies.)

❏ Check here if billing address is different from
shipping address and attach purchase order and
billing address information.

Signature_____

❏ **PAYMENT ENCLOSED: $**_____

❏ **PLEASE CHARGE TO MY CREDIT CARD.**

❏ Visa ❏ MasterCard ❏ AmEx ❏ Discover
❏ Diner's Club ❏ Eurocard ❏ JCB

Account # _____

Exp. Date_____

Signature_____

Prices in US dollars and subject to change without notice.

NAME_____

INSTITUTION_____

ADDRESS_____

CITY_____

STATE/ZIP_____

COUNTRY_____ COUNTY (NY residents only)_____

TEL_____ FAX_____

E-MAIL_____

May we use your e-mail address for confirmations and other types of information? ❏ Yes ❏ No
We appreciate receiving your e-mail address and fax number. Haworth would like to e-mail or fax special
discount offers to you, as a preferred customer. **We will never share, rent, or exchange your e-mail address
or fax number.** We regard such actions as an invasion of your privacy.

Order From Your Local Bookstore or Directly From
The Haworth Press, Inc.
10 Alice Street, Binghamton, New York 13904-1580 • USA
TELEPHONE: 1-800-HAWORTH (1-800-429-6784) / Outside US/Canada: (607) 722-5857
FAX: 1-800-895-0582 / Outside US/Canada: (607) 722-6362
E-mail: getinfo@haworthpressinc.com
PLEASE PHOTOCOPY THIS FORM FOR YOUR PERSONAL USE.
www.HaworthPress.com

BOF00